Shifter 3: Dedrick's Taming

By
Jaden Sinclair

Published by
Melange Books, LLC
White Bear Lake, MN 55110
www.melange-books.com

Shifter 3, Dedrick's Taming - Jaden Sinclair, Copyright © 2010, 2011
ISBN 978-1-61235-029-5

Names, characters, and incidents depicted in this book are products of the author's imagination or are used fictitiously. Any resemblance to actual events, locales, organizations, or persons, living or dead, is entirely coincidental and beyond the intent of the author or the publisher. No part of this book may be reproduced or transmitted in any form or by any means, electronic or mechanical, including photocopying, recording, or by any information storage and retrieval system, without permission in writing from the publisher.

Credits
Editor: Nancy Schumacher
Copy Editor: Taylor Evans
Format Editor: Mae Powers
Cover Artist: Caroline Andrus

Shifter 3: Dedrick's Taming
Jaden Sinclair

Dedrick Draeger is on edge. He has been the rock of the family, bearing the bunt of all responsibilities. But now the rock is starting to crumble and Dedrick is afraid for the first time in his life. Afraid of what fate has in store for him. Dedrick has been Jaclyn Davis's fantasy come true, and ignoring the warnings she gives into her desire. One night in his arms is all it took, but what neither of them realized is, the one night started something. Dedrick has his mate, but is Jaclyn ready for the big bad wolf?

Dedication:

This one is for all you readers out there who have been waiting for the big bad wolf. Enjoy! And Pat Sager, thanks again for all the help and support. Even though I make you cry in a book or two, you still come back for more.

www.jadensinclair.com

Interplanetary Passions
Outerplanetary Sensations
The Proposal
S.E.T.H.
S.H.I.L.O.
Lucifer's Lust, with Mae Powers
Shifter 1-7

Shifter 3: Dedrick's Taming
Jaden Sinclair

Chapter One

Jaclyn Davis stood outside the airport terminal, her foot tapping as she waited for her ride to show up. Several times now, she had looked down the road with the hopes that her ride was coming. After calling the Draeger house to check on Sidney again, she had been told that Adrian was coming to get her, not Dedrick. Which sucked! She wanted him to be the one picking her up. Wanted to see him again.

Jaclyn knew that she shouldn't chase after a man like that, or in this case a wolf. She had always been attracted to him. For whatever crazy reason, the moment she found out he was a wolf, it only made her attraction to him much more fierce.

Yes, she should stay away from him. She tried like hell to keep it in mind. But Sidney always had a reason for her to come for a visit here. Now, Jaclyn was in town while her best friend had her first baby or children as it was. She was expecting twins.

Jaclyn wasn't the kind of woman to ever stay in one place too long. When she saw how fatal an attraction could become, she tended to run as far away as she could. Yet, here she was once again, about to walk into the lion's den, while hoping to fight the desire she had for Dedrick Draeger.

It was a mistake. Her gut was screaming for her to run. If she stayed here too long this time, Jaclyn had no way of knowing if she could ever get out again, at least not whole. As much as she loved her best friend, this family was slowly wrapping around her heart. Jaclyn didn't know how to tell Sidney things were finally changing for her. She was afraid to face Dedrick or his family again. Afraid they would see what she had been hiding for so long.

"Come on, Adrian," she mumbled to herself. "Where the hell are you?"

She hated having to stand here waiting. It gave her too much time to think. She hated having to think. When her mind wandered, memories of how screwed up her own family had been or the crap her mother pulled on her for so many years, came rushing back.

To this day, Jaclyn still hadn't told Sidney the real reason why she went back to see her mother months ago. Sure, she shrugged it off, made everyone think it wasn't anything important. Just her mother mooching some money out of her, kind of thing. The real story was that Lucy Davis had been dying. Her mother had cancer. She was being eaten up inside. Because Lucy was dying, she had felt all guilty over the life she had given her only daughter. Jaclyn wasn't very forgiving, but she had stayed with her mother until the end.

Her cell phone went off in her pocket, which snapped Jaclyn from her memories. "Hello!"

"Sidney wanted me to call you again. Where are you?"

Jaclyn rolled her eyes looking once more down the road. "I'm still at the airport waiting, Sky. Your man hasn't shown up yet."

Skyler Draeger, or Laswell now, was the baby of the family. About nine months ago, she had mated with Adrian Laswell, which started real rocky. After the night he placed his claim on her, Skyler had caught him bumping uglies with her best friend. It didn't go over very well at the beginning, but it ended great.

"Now explain to me again why she isn't in a hospital?" Jaclyn demanded, her patience slipping away quickly. Sidney was like a sister to her. She didn't like the idea of her giving birth to the twins at the house.

"It's not safe." Skyler sighed on the other line. "Stefan feels like her father might try something."

Jaclyn snorted. "Please. He isn't going to come out of the woodwork now, if he hasn't already."

"You may be right, Jaclyn. But we still need to keep her safe. Twin births rarely happen with full shifter females. For Sidney, a human, to be doing it is like a borderline miracle."

Jaclyn could hear the worry in Skyler's voice. It scared the shit out of her. If something happened to Sidney, she didn't think she would ever be able to forgive Stefan, or any of them for that matter.

"What kind of car am I looking for again?"

"Four door, black Ford truck," Skyler answered. "He had to have it after the transmission went out in his other one.

Jaclyn strained her neck over a small crowd of people who were trying to get the attention of a cabbie. She saw what she thought was a black truck, but in the dark, it was hard to say. "I think he might be here, finally."

Sure enough, a black Ford truck skidded to a stop right in front of her. The passenger window rolled down. A smiling Adrian was leaning across the seat. "Hey, gorgeous, need a lift?"

"He's here, Sky." Jaclyn gave Adrian her I'm-bored expression. "Tell Sid we're on our way." She hung the phone up, went over to the truck, and leaned against the door. "You're late."

"No, you're early," he stated, his cheerful grin in place as always. "I was told your plane didn't land until six, to be here by ten after." He looked at his wristwatch. "Ten after on the dot."

Jaclyn rolled her eyes while opening the door. "Whatever." She shoved her backpack over the seat into the back and grabbed his wrist as she did. "It's six thirty!"

Adrian glanced at his watch, then back at her with his mouth agape. "Well, how about that."

Jaclyn started to see red, yanked the thing right off his wrist, and tossed it out the window. "Now it's gone."

"Hey! Dedrick gave me that for my birthday," he complained.

Jaclyn crossed her arms over her chest and stared straight ahead. "Well he needs better taste. It sucked. Now drive."

"Boy, we are testy tonight."

They drove in silence. When the airport was far behind them, she spoke again. "So how is she really?"

The *she* Jaclyn was referring to was Sidney. From the frown on Adrian's face, she knew he was just as worried as she was.

"They're early." Adrian kept his eyes on the road. "The doctor says it's natural for twins to come early. They appear to be a good size." He finally turned and smiled. "They are half shifter, so don't worry about them not coming out just fine."

"I'm more worried about Sidney." Jaclyn sighed. "Last time she called me, she said the doctor had put her on bed rest."

Adrian nodded. "Yeah, she was starting to get pretty swollen and eating a lot of shit." He chuckled as if he was recalling a funny memory. It hit Jaclyn then how much of this pregnancy thing she had missed out on. "Between Natasha cooking all day and Stefan running for midnight snacks, it's no wonder she started to swell."

"But how is she now?" Jaclyn was a little more forceful in her question.

Adrian sighed. "The labor is hard right now. Her water broke at two in the morning. We called you a couple hours or so afterward. When I left to pick you up, I think she was still only dilated to about four or five. So slow would be your answer."

"Great." Jaclyn groaned, slumping back in the seat. "You guys should have taken her to a hospital."

"The doc has brought in extra hands. Everything she is going to need, including the thingy in the back for pain. Its all there for her. She's going to be fine." He gave her hand a quick squeeze. "Now Stefan on the other hand is a nervous wreck!"

"Good." She snorted again. "Serves him right for getting her pregnant so fast."

"Dedrick's nervous as well."

Jaclyn knew just by his tone that Adrian was testing a ground she didn't want to go to right now. She put on her best I-don't-care face when she turned in her seat to face Adrian. "I don't recall asking about him."

Adrian smiled, and laughed. "Oh, but I know better. See, while everyone was fixed on my problem with Skyler, I saw how you acted around Dedrick."

"Adrian, you don't know jack shit." She gave him a push as she straightened in her seat. "And you saw even less. Dedrick isn't interested in me anymore than I am in him."

"Sure." He drew the word out. Jaclyn told herself it didn't matter what he thought. She wasn't here for Dedrick, him or anyone else in the house but for Sidney. "Save that lie for someone who knows better."

For the rest of the trip, they were silent. With each mile that went by, Jaclyn was starting to feel like she was the one having the babies. She was so antsy to be at the house that she felt like screaming. When the double iron gates came into view, she let out a breath she hadn't realized she was holding.

Before the truck had even stopped completely, Jaclyn had the door open and was out racing for the front door. She didn't knock or wait for Adrian. No, Jaclyn walked right in as if she lived in the house with everyone else.

Right off, she could feel the tension. It was so thick she thought she could cut it with a knife. It was surprisingly quiet. Jaclyn thought it was strange that if a woman were in hard labor, there would be screaming and all kind of panic in the house. Yet, she heard none of that.

"Where's everyone at?" she asked as soon as Adrian joined her in the open hallway right in front of the staircase.

"Good question," Adrian answered. "Hello! I'm back!"

"Jaclyn!" Natasha came out of the front room off to the side with a kind smile on her face. As always, she appeared like the lady of the house with her black slacks and silk top. "Sidney has been asking for you for hours now." She gave Adrian a quick look before hugging Jaclyn. "I'm glad you're back."

Shifter 3, Dedrick's Taming - Jaden Sinclair

Jaclyn hugged Natasha and wished for the hundredth time that this could have been her mother instead of the one she was born with. For a wolf, Natasha was one hell of a gentle lady.

"How's she doing?" Jaclyn asked, pulling out of the embrace. "Really?"

Natasha took a deep breath and smiled quickly. "So far it's been hard. Dr. Sager is in the kitchen talking to Stefan. She just gave her an epidural, so Sidney is resting now and letting nature do its thing." She rubbed Jaclyn's arms. "Skyler is up with her now and I know Sidney will be thrilled to see you."

"I'll just take this up to your room," Adrian said, brushing past Jaclyn, with her backpack in his hand.

"Oh . . . wait," she tried to call out.

"No waiting this time," Natasha cut in. "Your room is all ready, and I expect you to stay longer this time than a few weeks here and there." Natasha hooked her arm into Jaclyn's. Turning her around, Natasha walked up the stairs with her.

"Natasha, really." Jaclyn tried to shake off her uneasy feeling with a laugh. "I didn't bring many clothes with me. I didn't plan for a long, extended stay."

"Clothes can be replaced," Natasha stated with a pat to Jaclyn's hand. "Time can't." She walked Jaclyn right up to Sidney's bedroom and stopped. "You mean a lot to Sidney, and regardless of what other members in this household think, you have a place within this family."

Jaclyn couldn't stop the smile. Of all the people she had met over the years, Natasha Draeger was a one of a kind woman. It was another reason Jaclyn didn't like staying at the house too long. Natasha had a way of making her feel like she really was a part of this family.

They stopped at the bedroom door just as Skyler was coming out of the room. Skyler Draeger Laswell was a very pretty girl. Her brown hair was now cut short, just touching her shoulders, and her blue eyes held the bright sparkle of youth. Being married—or mated—as they called it, seemed to be agreeing with her. Skyler was always a breath of fresh air and sunshine when she entered any room, except that time she wanted to kill Adrian for mating her.

"You made it!" Skyler rushed up to Jaclyn and hugged her. This was another thing that Jaclyn wasn't used to, all this affection being shown to her.

"Yeah, teach Adrian to tell time, will ya." Jaclyn chuckled, pulling out of her arms. "Oh, and he needs a new watch." Both Skyler and Natasha frowned. Jaclyn shrugged. "Sort of tossed it out the window."

Skyler smiled and covered her mouth with her hand. "Don't tell Dedrick that." She lowered her hand. "He bought it for Adrian."

"How's she doing?" Natasha asked.

"Oh, the doc just went in to check on her progress," Skyler answered. When Jaclyn frowned, Skyler rolled her eyes and quickly went on. "Dr. Sager. She is a shifter doctor and has been taking care of Sidney since we first learned about the babies. She put Sidney on bed rest for the last few weeks. Stefan has been doing *everything*, including carrying her to the bathroom. But Sidney got up in the middle of the night to go without waking him, and her water broke. He's pissed over it."

"Well, he'll get over it fast enough." Jaclyn stepped around Skyler.

Jaclyn knocked then walked inside. Dr. Sager was just finishing her exam and smiled at Jaclyn. Jaclyn met Sidney's eyes and she rushed over to the bed. There she sat down on the side, and hugged Sidney tightly.

"Oh, I've missed you." Jaclyn groaned, tightening her hold on Sidney.

"Why do you stay away so damn long?" Sidney started to cry in her arms and Jaclyn felt guilt wash over her. Only tears from Sidney could force her to stay or go.

"Well, you know—" Jaclyn pulled back, brushing some of Sidney's hair from her damp forehead. "—Places to see, guys to nail." Sidney laughed, and Jaclyn touched her belly. "Getting close I hear."

"Mrs. Draeger, you are now at seven centimeters," Dr. Sager said. "I think with the epidural in place you should be able to relax and have the babies in a couple of hours."

Jaclyn sat back, but she held onto Sidney's hands. It seemed that Sid needed the comfort, and it didn't bother her to give it.

"I'm scared, Jacy," Sidney whispered. "I'm so afraid about having them at this time. I…I think I made a mistake getting out of the bed." A single tear slipped from her eye, and Jaclyn quickly wiped it away. "It's still early for them. What if something goes wrong and…"

"Shhh." Jaclyn bent over and kissed her on the forehead while brushing her hair and wiping her tears away, one more time. "Don't think like that. I'm sure that if Stefan or anyone else thought something would go wrong, or the babies were in any danger, you would be in a hospital."

"I can't do this alone anymore." More tears fell from her eyes. "You are my family. I can't do the wife and mother thing and not have you with me to share it." She swallowed hard. "I've always shared everything with you.

Jaclyn grinned and gave her hand a squeeze. "Now don't bring out the guilt card, or you might make me start crying. I'm here, like I promised. So let's worry about having some kids and not on how long I'm going to stay. Okay?"

Sidney nodded and sighed. "I'm so tired."

Jaclyn looked at her best—her only friend. Sidney did look exhausted. How could she not be worried for her and the babies? She wondered if Sidney was going to have the strength to push when the time came. Someone—she suspected Skyler—had French braided Sidney's golden brown hair for her, but strands had worked their way loose during her long labor. Even Sidney's green eyes were dull from the strain, which made Jaclyn wish like hell she could take it all away for her.

"Hey." Stefan popped his head in the door. "Safe to come in?" He didn't wait for an answer. He came in and closed the door softly. Then he went to the other side of the bed, sat down, and took Sidney's hand.

Jaclyn watched as Stefan kissed Sidney's hand, then her cheek and forehead, and rested his own head against hers. It was a tender moment showing Jaclyn just how much he loved Sidney. It also brought out her own yearning, one that she had buried so long ago and forgot about.

"Forgive me," Stefan whispered. "I didn't mean to get angry with you."

Jaclyn stood and moved away from the bed. She felt uncomfortable being so close to a private moment. She didn't know why all of a sudden it made her feel this way. Jaclyn had watched many mushy moments between Stefan and Sidney, but for some reason, this one bothered her. Deep longing hit her. She wanted what they had, but couldn't bring herself to open her heart for it.

"Shit, they're coming!" Sidney yelled out, causing Jaclyn to jump.

She went back to the bed and dropped down to the floor on her knees. "Are you sure?"

"Look!" Sidney screamed.

Jaclyn stood up and tossed the blanket that was over Sidney to the side, moved the gown up, and looked between her legs. Her eyes widened when she saw the crown of a baby's head. "Stefan...um...you might want to get the doctor, like right now."

Stefan didn't ask questions. He let go of Sidney's hand and ran out of the room.

"Sidney, don't push," Jaclyn instructed her.

"I can't!" Sidney yelled again.

"Oh, shit!" Jaclyn quickly got on her knees on the bed and put Sidney's legs up on her shoulders. She didn't know what she was doing, but she did know she was about to catch a baby. "If this is your way of making me stay for the birth, all you had to do was ask, damn it!"

Sidney pushed, and Jaclyn waited. Little by little, the head squeezed out, and Jaclyn prayed the doctor would come back before it was completely out.

Stefan and the doctor came in just when Sidney pushed the head out. Dr. Sager didn't move Jaclyn aside, as she hoped, but instead stood off to the side, assisting her. She sucked the nose and mouth out quickly, then told Sidney to push again once she was ready. Dr. Sager told Jaclyn to take hold of the head and help guide the baby out as she got a clamp ready.

Sidney screamed one last time with her push as the baby came out and Jaclyn smiled. There was no way in hell she would have even thought she would be the one to help her best friend deliver a baby.

"It's a boy!" Jaclyn cried, tears falling freely.

Dr. Sager had also brought along two nurses. She clamped the cord, Jaclyn moved out of the way, and the baby, screaming all the way, was quickly handed over to a nurse who carried the baby from the bed to a basinet. Jaclyn moved over to watch the baby. He seemed so small but sounded so very strong.

"The second baby is coming down nicely," Dr. Sager said. "Shouldn't be much longer now, and we will have number two!"

"Jacy, how is he?" Sidney asked, sounding weak and tired.

Jaclyn took the baby from the nurse and went to Sidney. She knelt on the floor to let Sidney have a look. "Perfect. Wouldn't you say, Dad?"

Stefan acted as if he was afraid to touch the baby. "Oh, Sidney," he moaned.

"Okay, here comes number two," Dr. Sager announced.

Jaclyn turned and handed the baby back to the nurse and helped again. She took Sidney's other hand and held her leg up just as Stefan was doing.

She pushed and she pushed, and Jaclyn thought it was taking forever for number two to come. But like they say about light at the end of the tunnel, they had it when the doctor told them that the head was crowning.

Minutes seemed to drag by like hours as Sidney pushed the second baby out. With a quick announcement from the doctor, Sidney's second child was born.

"Another boy!" Dr. Sager smiled, holding the screaming baby up for all of them to see before handing it off to the second nurse. "Congratulations, Mrs. Draeger. I think you are the first human to give birth to twins that are half shifter and perfectly healthy." She smiled. "And they're two minutes apart by my watch and appear to have fine lungs. Good job, Mama!"

"Baby A, is five pounds, six ounces, and baby B is five pounds, three ounces," one of the nurses said.

"Sidney?" Jaclyn's gut dropped when she glanced from the babies to Sidney who was out cold.

"She's fine," Dr. Sager said, wiping her hands on a towel. "Just exhausted.

Jaclyn nodded and grinned. "You did good, girl," she whispered before kissing Sidney on the cheek. "I'm going to go tell the others."

Stefan nodded but didn't move from Sidney's side. Out in the hall, the whole family was waiting. Jaclyn looked each one of them in the eye and smiled big. "Twin boys."

Natasha, Skyler, and Adrian all rushed into the bedroom, but Dedrick lingered. He obviously wanted to talk.

"Sidney told me, the last time she called, what she was going to name them if they ended up being boys," Jaclyn said. "I think Drake Dedrick and Brockton Adrian are good names."

Dedrick nodded his head. "She made my mother cry with the honor of naming them after our father."

"And their uncles."

"Yeah, that was a bit of a surprise." Stuffing his hands into his jeans, he gave Jaclyn the impression that he was uncomfortable being around her.

"Jesus, Dedrick." Jaclyn sighed. "You act like I jumped your bones or something. It was a kiss. Get over it." She brushed past him to head toward her room. "Wasn't even a good one, anyway."

She didn't get far. Dedrick grabbed her arm, stopped her, and forced Jaclyn to take steps backward to face him again. "We're both adults here, Jaclyn. I'm sure I can trust you to act like one."

Jaclyn yanked her arm out of his hand. "Drop the grizzly bear act, Dedrick. Doesn't work for me, remember?" He growled low, and she grinned, crossing her arms over her chest. "And neither does that shit." She uncrossed her arms and poked him in the chest. "You seem to forget that I'm not the faint of heart where you're concerned. Your growling and barking doesn't scare me in the least."

warned with a low rumble.

"Or what?" She poked again. "You're going to go all alpha on my ass?"

He grabbed her wrist, yanked her close, and wrapped her arm behind her back. "You have no damn clue what you are doing." He spoke soft, but his voice was thick. "Don't try to learn what our kind is all about with *me*." He gave her another jerk, tightened his hold, and put a small amount of pressure on her arm, enough to have it throbbing with a bit of pain. "I'm not the one you want to play these fucking games with." He cocked his head to one side, eyes shifting back and forth between their normal dark to a deep red. "I could hurt you real bad."

Dedrick let her go so fast that Jaclyn stumbled. She watched as he walked by her, went into the bedroom with the others, and closed the door gently behind him. Jaclyn shook her head and headed down the hall to her room.

The bedroom assigned to her was one of their guest rooms. Natasha had told her many times that she could paint or hang up photos, and even Sidney had tried to get her to redo the room to her own tastes and standards, but Jaclyn couldn't do it. She felt that if she painted and hung pictures up, then it would become her home, and she couldn't do that. She couldn't settle down like Sidney wanted to. The price was too high.

Ever since she moved out of her mother's shitty apartment, Jaclyn had made herself a promise that she would never stay in one place for too long. She would never be found, no matter what, and she stuck to it. College was the only time she stayed in one place longer than a month, and it had almost cost her. It was just easier for her to move around, as well as letting Sidney think she liked to be on the move rather than it having to do with her safety.

Shaking the damn past off once again, she closed the bedroom door and headed for the bathroom. Her bag was on the bed, and she stopped at the foot to take her shoes off, but the rest came off in the bathroom.

She stripped, turned the shower on to a steamy hot, and stood under the water with her eyes closed, a sigh on her lips. Jaclyn stayed in the shower until the hot water started to get cold. She turned the spray off, grabbed the towel on the hook, and got out. Rolling her head on her shoulders, she glanced at the clock next to the bed and couldn't believe that it was already one in the morning. Where the hell had the time gone? Had she really been here close to seven hours now?

having fun," she said to herself.

Jaclyn went over to her bag to dig out her long silk robe. The one and only present her father had sent her—loose cotton shorts and one of her tight tank tops to sleep in. She dressed and slipped the robe on as she headed back for the door.

She had been in such a hurry to get to Sidney before she had the babies that she had forgotten to eat a thing, and now she was starving. The house was surprisingly quiet as she slipped into the hallway. She smiled when she walked past Sidney's door and heard the faint crying of a baby and Natasha giving orders.

Down the stairs, she went and into the dining room that led to the kitchen tucked in the back of the house. Jaclyn stopped when she saw Stefan and Adrian seated at the table drinking a beer. Adrian was the one who looked up and saw her, motioning for her to join them.

"Come on in!" Adrian smiled. "We always have room for one more to celebrate with."

"How's Sidney doing?" Jaclyn asked, looking at Stefan as she headed for the fridge. "Don't mind, do you?" She pointed to it before opening the door.

"Help yourself," Stefan answered. "Sid is sleeping, and my mother and sister are up there cleaning the babies as well as Sidney. They kicked me out of the room."

Jaclyn chuckled. "I can see that. Men tend to get in the way."

"Hey, you owe me a watch," Adrian said, giving her a small nudge when she walked past him with some lunchmeat.

"I'll make sure to buy you a digital one so you can read it," she teased back.

Stefan laughed. "So where you been this time?" he asked once she sat down with her sandwich.

"Nowhere special." Jaclyn shrugged. "Just spent some time in the mountains doing some skiing."

"Now that's where I should take Skyler." Adrian sat back in his chair with his arms crossed over his chest. "Skiing, late nights in front of the fire all toasty and warm with the snow falling around us."

"But you can't ski," Stefan said.

"Who said anything about *actually* skiing?" Adrian winked at Jaclyn.

"Is sex all you guys have on your minds?" she asked.

"Yes," they answered together.

Jaclyn laughed and shook her head. "One of you doesn't have a twin I could steal, do you?"

Adrian remarked, earning him a kick under the table from Stefan.

"What was that for?" Adrian whined, rubbing his leg.

Jaclyn glared at Adrian. After rolling her eyes and repeating to herself not to kill him or cause him bodily harm she turned to Stefan. "So are you going to take me back to the airport in a few days, or am I stuck with this idiot?" She thumbed in Adrian's direction.

Stefan shook his head no. "Not this time, honey. You're staying longer than a week."

"Stefan." She sighed.

"Sidney and Mom both have officially ganged up on you. On me, as well." He gave her a large smile that wasn't happy. "You have to stay at least until the party."

"But that's three months away!"

Jaclyn couldn't believe this was happening. She had only planned on doing her usual. Come, stay about a week, and then take off. It was a simple plan, one that worked great. She was friendly, but not overly attached to anyone in the house. The sad part of it was that each time she came back, she felt herself growing attached to them all over again. She loved being in the house, watching the playfulness of Adrian and Skyler, as well as how Sidney had wrapped Stefan around her finger. Watching them was the only way she was able to live this kind of life. But it was getting harder and harder to leave each time.

"Too bad." Stefan stood up and took her plate. "Skyler is going to take you shopping for some clothes and I don't want to hear it!" he snapped when she opened her mouth.

Jaclyn stood up as well and leaned on one foot in front of Stefan with her arms crossed over her chest. "Sidney has been working on you, hasn't she?"

Stefan also crossed his arms over his chest and grinned. "What if she has?"

"You are so pussy-whipped." She snorted.

Stefan pushed off the counter and kissed her quickly on the cheek. "Sweet dreams. I'm going to check on my wife. Night."

As soon as he was out of the kitchen, Jaclyn turned and hit Adrian as hard as she could on the side of the arm.

"What was that for?" he whined.

"Get it through that thick skull of yours, Adrian Laswell," she snapped. "Dedrick doesn't want anything to do with me, and I'm tired of trying. As soon as this damn party is over with, I'm gone, and I won't be coming back for long, cozy-ass visits." She hit him again. "So stop trying to push him on me. He's not interested."

from the table, but he had a smug expression on his face. "Keep telling yourself that one, but I know different. When the two of you are close, the sparks fly. If you're staying for three months, I *know* things are going to get very interesting around here. See you in the morning."

Jaclyn watched him leave the kitchen as well and glared at his back. "God, how did I get sucked into a three-month stay?" She groaned before going over to the light switch and turning it off. "I can't stay that long without fucking something up."

Chapter Two
Three months later

Martinis was one of the hottest and most difficult clubs to get into in the city. It was also a good two-hour drive for Dedrick to get to from the house. He parked on the side of the road, right across from the front door, and sighed. It had been months, maybe even a full year since the last time he had walked through those doors, yet here he was once again, only this time sex was not one of the things on his mind. No, this time he was on a mission, and it caused him to grind his teeth together.

Dedrick pushed his door open and got out of his car. He was dressed simply—tight jeans, sleeveless shirt that fit like a second skin, and shit-kicker boots. His dark hair blew in the breeze, and it wasn't long before the young girls standing in the line turned to watch him walk across the street to the front door.

At one time, Dedrick was a regular, so for him to get in the club, all he had to do was nod to the bouncer who moved aside and let him in without one question, kind of like now. The club was in full swing—music blasting, drinks flowing, and people were dancing and making out in corners—just as Dedrick remembered.

He scanned the place, and it was damn hard since it was packed to the max. Dedrick had planned to pick her up with his senses, but the place was too busy and too full of hundreds of sweaty bodies. So he used his eyes and looked at each girl who bore a similarity to Jaclyn. Just when he was about to give up, he found her.

Jaclyn was leaning over the bar and she was dressed to kill. She wore a black, leather mini skirt. It was skin tight and so short that it wouldn't take much for a guy to walk up and pull the thing up and get a nice hand full. Her long black hair was loose, caressing her backside when she moved. Black cowboy boots were on her feet and Dedrick caught glimpses of the loose white tank top she wore. It was a temptation he didn't need right now.

Before he went to work pushing his way through the crowd toward her, Dedrick steeled himself for the fighting that always seemed to come whenever they got close. He came up behind her, gave the guy she was talking to a hard glare before he ordered a shot of tequila and took a seat on the bar stool.

Jaclyn turned to him slowly, no expression on her face. "What do you want, Dedrick?" She took the drink that Dedrick had ordered, drank it down, hissed, and slammed the glass back on the bar. "Kind of busy here."

"Need to talk," Dedrick said, raising his finger for another drink.

"Need to talk," she repeated, nodding her head. "Bullshit! You want something." When she cocked her head to the left, her thick hair fell off her shoulder to brush his arm. "And what a surprise, I find myself not giving a shit."

"Jesus." He groaned, picked up the shot glass, and swallowed the liquor. "Do you think you could give me a break here?"

Jaclyn acted as if she were thinking real hard. "Nope."

She turned from him and was about to walk away when he grabbed her arm and yanked her toward him. "We need to come to an understanding here, Jaclyn. Sidney is my sister-in-law. Any kind of involvement with you will hurt her. I'm not going to do that to my brother."

"And there you are wrong once again," she snapped, inches from his face. She pulled her arm free but didn't move away. "Sidney has nothing to do with this. I make my own mistakes." Her gaze roamed over his body, and Dedrick felt something deep inside him stir. "Now, if you will excuse me, I'm going to try to take your advice and find some company that *fits* my kind."

Dedrick wasn't ready to let her go just yet. He wrapped his arms around her and, cupping her leather-covered ass with his hands, held her between his legs. "Now, Jaclyn." He lowered his voice, letting it purr. "I never pictured you to be a woman scorned before."

Jaclyn smiled sweetly, draped her arms over his shoulders, and leaned into him. "I'm not scorned, Dedrick, just not interested anymore. There's a big difference, and you need to learn it."

"You're interested," he told her, squeezing her ass to emphasize his words. "It comes off of you so strong, I can smell it."

"Well, then I guess I need to change my soap." She pried his hands from her ass and took a step back as he chuckled.

"Come on," Dedrick said, his voice lowering as he moved closer to her ear. "I see it in your eyes every time you look at me. You're very interested." She met his eyes in the mirror over the bar. "And curious," he whispered. "You're dying inside to know what having sex with me is all about."

Jaclyn pushed back against him and turned. "Curiosity killed many cats, and I don't have the lives to spare on you." She picked up another beer and took a deep drink. "Tell Sid I'll come by soon. And if she has to send someone to check on me, to please let it not be you."

Dedrick rubbed his face groaning at the same time. "Okay, what do you want?"

She turned her head, and her blue eyes grabbed his full attention, which made Dedrick feel like he could drown in them. "She must really have something on you if you can't go home without me."

"I don't want her upset," Dedrick stated. "It's that simple."

"Is that the only thing?" Jaclyn cocked her head to one side. As she did, her thick black hair spilled to the side too. It gave Dedrick a mental picture of all that black hair spilling over his chest and then over his legs.

"What do you want?" he said again, after clearing his throat and pushing the image of her sucking on his cock to the back of his mind.

Jaclyn turned back toward him, licked her lips, and gave him a shrug. "Doesn't really matter now."

"Oh, don't chicken out on me now." He grinned, licked his own lips, and set the bottle down on the bar. "You might have me change my opinion of you."

She snorted, rolling her eyes and snatching her beer back. "Please. Your opinion of me means jack shit." She moved closer and stood between his legs, her scent wrapping around him. "You don't like me. You've made that very clear, and now that I know you don't want a human, it kind of makes my next request pointless."

"Do you always like to flirt with danger?" His voice was raw and sounded on edge. He raised his hand to wrap some of her long hair into his fist.

"I tend to get bored easily," she answered quietly.

"Cut the shit, Jaclyn." He growled low, tugging on her hair. "What do you want?"

She moved closer, hanging her arms over his shoulders once more, pressing closer to his body. "I want you to kiss me again." She licked her lips and dropped her gaze to his mouth. "Like a lover would kiss me."

Dedrick felt his gut drop. Of all the things for her to ask of him, that was not what he had expected. Dedrick wouldn't lie to himself. He did think Jaclyn was hot, and kissing her again would probably be great, but what door would it open? What would the consequences be if he kissed Jaclyn the way she wanted? He didn't want to give her false hope or to start something with her that he had no intention of finishing. Dedrick had meant what he had said. He didn't mess around with humans. Period.

"If I kiss you, will you come home for Sidney?" His cock was so hard he thought he was going to burst through his zipper.

"If you kiss me right, and I mean if you hold nothing back, then yes," she panted.

"Okay." He took a deep breath. "But before I do this, I want you to understand something. Nothing changes between us."

"Understood."

Dedrick fisted more of her hair and brought her face down closer to his. Since she was standing and he was sitting on a bar stool, she hovered over him. He touched her cheek with his free hand. Her skin was so soft for someone who seemed to act so tough to the world.

Dedrick moved his hand from her cheek down to her throat felt the pulse of her excitement. He could smell it in the air. Jaclyn was a drug to his system, one that, if he wasn't careful, he could become addicted to. Dedrick's cock throbbed behind his jeans. He questioned the sanity in his actions when a painful need hit him. Dedrick couldn't explain why, but when it came to Jaclyn, he was weak and ready to give her anything she asked for, just like his damn dick was hard to be inside her.

"One taste," Dedrick mumbled before his lips touched hers.

It started off slow and easy, just two sets of lips brushing against each other. Much too suddenly, it all changed. Jaclyn pressed closer, her fingers digging into his hair and tugging, her nails scraping his scalp. The slight pain was enough to get him all worked up and to make things change from a simple kiss to one that quickly became demanding.

Dedrick released her hair and dug both hands into the flesh of her ass, grinding her even closer between his legs, letting her feel his stiff cock. Slanting his head, he deepened the kiss. It was pure, raw hunger. Somehow, Dedrick managed to get Jaclyn to spread her legs and ride his leg. He moved his tongue, slipping it inside her mouth, and Jaclyn accepted it willingly. Sucking on it, she moaned her pleasure, and still Dedrick tried to kiss her deeper and harder.

"Motherfucker!" Dedrick sat up in his bed. His sheet was all wet and sweaty, besides being all tangled around his body. He was breathing hard, his cock a torturous throb between his legs from the dream he'd just had. "Argh!" he cried when he rolled over to his side and the head of his cock touched the sheet. It was so sensitive that the damn thing hurt.

Dedrick glanced at the clock next to his bed. Three in the morning, and he had gone to bed at midnight. Great! Three hours of sleep again, and another damn dream about kissing Jaclyn. Last dream he had, he almost fucked her. This one was only a kiss. "God, I need to get laid."

onto the bed. He only had three more hours before he had to be up to get ready for the yearly party, another thing Dedrick wasn't looking forward to.

Getting out of bed, Dedrick headed to the bathroom and took a quick, cool shower. He dressed in jeans and a T-shirt, and then headed down the stairs to find an early drink. Because it was three in the morning, he was somewhat surprised when he went downstairs and found Stefan, sitting at the table with a bowl of cereal in front of him, alone.

"Boys keeping you two up again?" Stefan jumped when Dedrick spoke. "Sorry, didn't mean to scare you."

"Yeah." Stefan sighed. "The boys and Sidney." He met Dedrick's eyes, and Dedrick saw the worry in his brother's eyes as well as the exhaustion. "She's crying again. Damn." Stefan groaned, pushed his bowl away, and rubbed his face. "This postpartum depression sucks."

"Did you call the doctor?" Even though it was too early to be drinking, Dedrick went over to the fridge and took out a beer. He was feeling the lingering affects of his dream, and his dick was still slightly hard.

"Yeah. I'm going to pick up some new medicine for her as soon as the pharmacy opens." Stefan stood and put his bowl in the sink. "She's in with Jaclyn, sleeping." Stefan kept his back to Dedrick, but it didn't take a genius to hear the pain in Stefan's voice. "I don't think she wants to sleep with me anymore."

"She's just adjusting," Dedrick said. "Give her time."

Stefan nodded but still didn't turn around. "I thought it was over last month, and then it came back." He swung around fast, and Dedrick couldn't believe he was seeing his brother crying. "She's hurting, man, and I can't . . ."

Dedrick moved toward Stefan and pulled him into his arms. It had been years since Dedrick had had to hold his little brother and let him cry on his shoulder. But for a shifter, to have his mate reject him, for whatever reason, was difficult. It was also hard for a human to give birth to half shifter children. Humans went through postpartum depression. Shifter females didn't.

"She's not rejecting you." Dedrick sighed, holding Stefan tightly. "Keep in mind Sidney is human, and it's natural for her to go through this." Dedrick took hold of Stefan's face and made him look at him. "It will run its course, and Sidney will be right back to chewing your ass out for something."

Stefan nodded. "You're right."

course I'm right, and if you tell anyone I hugged you, I'm going to kick your ass."

"Then I should have taken a picture." Adrian was smiling, leaning against the doorframe with his arms crossed over his chest. "It was definitely a Kodak moment."

"God, doesn't anyone in this house sleep!" Dedrick growled. He went back to the table and sat down with a sigh, picked his beer up and downed almost half of it.

"Not when you have two screaming boys," Adrian answered. "They're up again, and Skyler went in."

Stefan groaned. "I better get up there and check on them."

Adrian didn't move when Stefan walked past him. His eyes were on Dedrick, and Dedrick felt it. "What's on your mind, Adrian?"

Dedrick kept his eyes on his brother-in-law as he strolled over to the table and sat down across from him. "I want to know how long you're going to go around the house acting like she isn't here."

Dedrick rolled his eyes and groaned. "Damn it, Adrian. I don't need to have you lecture me. I have enough problems as it is." He stood up with every intention of leaving, but Adrian's voice stopped him.

"It isn't going to take much to crack that shell you have around yourself," Adrian said. "If she pushes hard enough, are you going to be able to fight it, really?" Dedrick glared over his shoulder at Adrian. "Look at you." Adrian raised his hands up and down. "You're not sleeping. You hide out in the damn pool house all the time, and the moment she comes into the room, you make up any excuse to leave. That shit isn't going to last forever."

"Stay out of it, Adrian," Dedrick warned him. "I'll be fine as soon as she leaves. I always am."

Adrian stood and pushed the chair in harder than he needed to. "Don't bet on it. One day, Dedrick, you are going to lose the one thing that means the world to you, and nothing will ever bring it back. Don't piss this one away," he said before storming out of the kitchen.

* * * *

The party was in full bloom. Shifters of all ages walked around the grounds of the Draeger home smiling, laughing, and greeting old and new friends. Jaclyn was amazed at how many humans she saw at the party—the party Sidney had demanded she stay here for.

Three long months she had stayed at the Draeger home helping with the children, helping Sidney, and just plain going crazy. She felt very out of place. It was the first time she had ever stayed in the house longer than a week or two, and she couldn't wait to take off again if for the house was getting very thick. Jaclyn felt like she needed some action and going to Martinis all the time wasn't dealing with it. What she really needed was a man, but for some damn reason, her body wouldn't let her have just anyone. No! It wanted a certain specimen of the male sex—one that wanted nothing to do with her.

Looking around at all the people, Jaclyn felt as if she were a twenty-five-year-old human in a den of beasts. The only problem she had was that in the time she'd been here, the beast she wanted was doing everything he could to stay the hell away from her.

Dedrick Draeger. His name alone spoken in the night gave her chills, caused her pussy to cream, and her clit to throb in need. He was her fantasy, her desire, and the one guy she should run as far away from as she could get.

Despite knowing what she should do, she couldn't run at all. Sure, she had kissed him, but it had been just a small peck. It had meant nothing to either of them, yet somehow it started something inside her. These feelings were starting to affect her in more ways than she wanted to admit. Attraction was one thing, but what Jaclyn felt each time she saw Dedrick or dreamed about him was another. Simply put, in her eyes, he was hot. No, what she wondered was if she was starting to crave what she couldn't have. Men did it all the time, so why couldn't a woman? Why couldn't she want what she wasn't supposed to have?

Jaclyn was dressed in an elegant skirt of creamy silk that Natasha and Sidney had given her with a matching loose top that was open on her back down to her waist. Her hair was in a loose bun on top of her head, with ringlets falling around her face. As much as she hated being all dressed up, Jaclyn had to admit that she looked good tonight. Now the trick was to get the attention of one man, and her goal would be complete. Jaclyn figured that one night of hot sex would be enough to get him out of her system, and then she could move on. At least she could if she could get her hands on him.

Why do you look so damn tense?" Sidney sneaked up behind Jaclyn and handed her a glass of wine over her shoulder.

Jaclyn took the glass, turned around, and smiled. Jaclyn drank half of the wine before answering. "I'm fine. You know I hate being dressed up is all." She frowned. "Are you supposed to be drinking that with your medicine?"

"Give me a break." Sidney rolled her eyes, looking around the grounds. "You're looking for Dedrick, and yes, I can have a glass."

Jaclyn snorted. "Please. The guy can't stand the sight of me." She peered around one more time before she returned her attention to can take these shoes off." She glanced down at her feet and shook her head. "Why did I let you talk me into heels?"

Sidney laughed. "Take the shoes off. No one is going to notice. And for a girl who has her eyes on him all the time, you sure are blind." Sidney moved her eyes up and down. "And you have the legs for heels."

"I'm not blind, and I don't have my eyes on him." Jaclyn defended herself, but she couldn't deny or hide her interest when Dedrick walked out of the house with Adrian.

"Yeah, right." Sidney snorted. "You're not interested at all." Sidney took hold of her wrist, making Jaclyn tear her eyes away from Dedrick to stare back at her. "Stay away from him, Jacy. He isn't the kind of guy you should mess with, and with the full moon at the end of the month Dedrick could become dangerous."

"I'm not going to do anything stupid, Sid." Jaclyn smiled. "Promise." Stefan caught her eye and she nodded in his direction. "Why don't you go to your husband and fix things with him. Stefan looks a bit lost."

Jaclyn watched Sidney walk over to Stefan, and she turned her attention back to Dedrick who was talking to Adrian. She could see he was tense and grumpy from the way he was walking and frowning at Adrian. She frowned herself when she saw Adrian toss his arms up in the air, point at Dedrick, and say something in anger. It was the first time she'd seen them fight since Skyler had come home and embraced her claiming.

From what Jaclyn had learned about his kind, she knew that his heat thing was starting to take its toll on him. Stefan even told her that the only way Dedrick was going to get any peace was when he found his mate. A part of Jaclyn wished she could be the one he needed. She would love to be protected by a man like Dedrick, and it would be even better to have that man in bed with her each and every night.

For three months, she had watched him retreat to the pool house, away from the family and her, especially her. The bickering that went on between them no longer existed, not even one smartass remark, and it hurt a lot. Jaclyn saw interest in his eyes. It was hidden all the time from her, but she still saw it when she was lucky to catch his eyes. She saw fear and hesitancy and knew it had to do with her being a human. Well, the time had come for Jaclyn to show Dedrick how strong this human really was and just how little he scared her! Just one taste of the candy from the jar was all she wanted, and then she would go on her merry way.

walked past one of the tables that had drinks on it, grabbed two bottles of beer while Dedrick stood and talked to Natasha. Looking around to see if anyone might be staring at her, Jaclyn left the party and headed down the path to the pool house.

The pool house was dark. Perfect for what Jaclyn wanted. She slipped inside and looked around, smiling when she closed the door. The place was a mess, but it wasn't quite as bad as some of the places she had stayed. It was large with two rooms and no kitchen. A daybed sat against the far wall with a large television in front of it, one overstuffed chair, a small fridge, and then the bathroom off to the right. The bed was a mess, clothes were all over the floor, and Jaclyn could smell the faint scent of Dedrick's cologne.

Jaclyn kicked her shoes off and tossed them off to the side. She walked around the room, picked up one of his shirts, and inhaled his scent. *Damn, he smells good.* She closed her eyes in bliss.

Holding both bottles with one hand, Jaclyn pulled the pins from her hair and let her long locks fall around her shoulders to brush at her lower back. Jaclyn walked to the back of the house while twisting the caps off the beer. She found a corner hidden in by shadows and waited for her dream to come walking in.

She didn't have long to wait. About five minutes later, Dedrick came strolling into the house, pulling at his tie. It felt like her heart was going to burst from her chest, and she couldn't stop the throbbing between her legs or the dampness that touched her panties. She kept an eye on him with stilled breath while he undressed before her eyes.

"Bullshit," he mumbled to himself.

His back was to her, but that was fine. Jaclyn didn't mind watching the backside of a hot guy, especially one like Dedrick. He took off his suit jacket and tossed it onto the chair. He yanked open his shirt with extra force, and Jaclyn had to bite her lip to still the noise that escaped her when it slid down his arms into the pile on the floor. Dedrick was all muscle—one big brick of it that flexed with his movements.

Dedrick kicked his shoes off, bent over to remove his socks, and then went to work on his slacks. Jaclyn felt more of her juices pool between her legs and soak her panties. There was something raw, untamed about him that had her wanting to sink to her knees and give him everything she had to give. His pants dropped, strong legs stepped out, and Jaclyn lost her cool and made a slight gasping sound. He stilled.

"I was wondering how long it was going to take for you to make a sound." Dedrick turned around and looked right in her direction, his each and every ripple from his chest down to his straining cock hidden inside his tight briefs. "For you, that was surprisingly quiet."

Jaclyn came out from her corner and handed the extra beer to him, her mouth open and tongue skimming over her teeth. "Don't stop on my account." Soaking in the sight of him, she took a drink. "The show's not over yet."

Dedrick took the beer from her and downed half of it. His eyes never left hers or changed in color. "And what show might that be?"

"You know what I've been wondering?" She strolled closer, taking in his male scent and feeling the heat from his body. She couldn't get over how much heat came off of him, how dangerous he seemed and how safe it all felt.

"What?" He growled the word, and it was enough to have more of her juices seeping out.

"Do you feel as hard as you try to act?" She moved close to him and looked up at his face. She reached out, gently touching his bare chest, smiling when he jumped from the contact. "Ahh, so you do." She reached for his beer and placed both bottles on a small table next to the bed. Jaclyn circled Dedrick, touching his arms, his back, down to his taut ass and then moved back around to his chest. "You're tense." She stared back up at him. She was glad when he lowered his head to her as if he might kiss her again. "Why is that?" The question came out in a mere whisper. "And why are you avoiding me?"

"You're playing a dangerous game." The words rumbled softly from his lips, but Dedrick didn't kiss her. His long hair brushed her face. He was so close. "You should leave before things get out of hand."

Jaclyn grinned, placed both hands on his chest, and raked her nails down. "I'm not playing any games." She pushed him and Dedrick fell back on the daybed. "Yet."

She stood between his legs staring down at him. His cock strained against his briefs and Jaclyn fought as much as she could not to ravish him, as she wanted to. It had been so long since she had had a man in her bed, and from what she was looking at now, this man was a walking sex machine.

"You should leave before things get out of hand," he reminded her, his deep voice thick and rough when he spoke. His arms came up, and his hands closed around the bars of the daybed. "You might start something you can't handle."

Jaclyn bent over and licked his chest down to his belly button, bit at his stomach before dropping down to her knees, which brought forth know what I'm doing, just like I'm damn sure I can handle you with no problem." Jaclyn took hold of the elastic band of his briefs and pulled them down. Dedrick helped by rising up for her. He tightened his hands on the bar, making his knuckles turn white. When Jaclyn glanced up at him, his eyes were half closed, bright red, and full of lust. "Very nice," she uttered when his cock sprang free before her eyes, thick, hard, and full of life. "And very impressive."

She took hold of his cock and stroked it as a lover would, tenderly. She watched his face, saw the pleasure that her touch was giving him and bent over once more to kiss, lick, and nibble his chest. Her mouth traveled down his flat, washboard chest to his stomach and even lower. His breathing increased, and Jaclyn could feel the tension rise in his body. She knew that finally, she had this beast right where she wanted him.

"How long has it been for you?" she asked. Her stare was drawn to his red eyes, and she licked the underside of his shaft to the crest of the head, then circled her tongue around the tiny slit that was coated with pre-come. "I find it hard to believe that a man like you"—she sucked on the head of his cock, which brought forth another hiss from him—"hasn't had a woman in months." She licked down the base to his scrotum, and then sucked the sac into her mouth.

"Oh shit!" Dedrick moaned.

Jaclyn looked up and smiled. He closed his eyes, and his hands fisted and unfisted on the bars of the bed. Jaclyn continued to lick at his thick cock, suck the head, not the base, before kissing and sucking her way back down to tease and please his heavy sack. His flesh pulsated in her mouth. His breathing increased almost to a pant and still, Jaclyn pleasured him.

"Would you like for me to stop?" She toyed with him but not with her tongue alone, but with her words. She swirled her tongue over the head before kissing it, and he answered her with a deep growl. "Oh, I do love it when you growl." She kissed her way back down the base, flicked her tongue around his balls before licking back up. "But this time you have to tell me if you want me to suck your dick."

He moved fast, fisting her long hair into his hand. Jaclyn felt her pulse quicken at the dark expression on his face. "What the fuck do you think?" he snarled, sounding deadly.

She smiled at him, reached up to his fist in her hair, and forced him to let go. Then she opened her mouth and took his throbbing cock deep into her mouth. Dedrick growled then quickly moaned. Sucking on the thick flesh, she marveled over how it stretched her lips to an almost painful point and found that she was dying to know how it would feel stretching her pussy.

He was so thick, and so long that there was no way she was going to be able to put all of him inside her mouth, but hell if she wasn't going to try. Jaclyn bobbed her head up and down, sucking on the hot flesh. With her tongue, she could feel the pulse, and with his moaning as well as bucking under her, she knew his orgasm was close. The swearing he did under his breath was another thing telling her how much he was fighting not to come.

Harder and faster, she moved on him, using her hand to stroke what she couldn't get into her mouth while the other hand cupped and massaged his balls. Finally, she thought, finally she had her fantasy under her, and she loved every moment of it.

Jaclyn moaned around him. Her clit throbbed. She was hot, wet, and in desperate need to have him inside her. Jaclyn wasn't too sure if she could hold out and give him what he needed, but she damn well was going to try.

"I can smell you." Dedrick snarled, his hips bucking under her mouth. "Son of a bitch. Your scent!"

Jaclyn popped his cock out of her mouth and moved her hand up and down the base as fast as she could. "And what are you going to do about it?" she taunted him by grazing her teeth over the sensitive head. When he stared at her, his eyes blazed red, and his face looked dark, almost primal. Jaclyn barely held back a whimper. She brought her index finger up to her lips and sucked the digit into her mouth. When she brought it out, it was nice and wet. "Are you ready?"

Before he could answer, she sucked his cock back into her mouth. Without giving him a warning, she took her index finger and pushed it as far as she could into his ass. Dedrick yelled and exploded in her mouth. He tensed under her, and stream after stream of his rich seed shot out. Jaclyn drank it down like a hungry kitten.

Dedrick was still breathing hard when Jaclyn released him, stood, grabbed her beer, and strolled back over to the corner she had been in earlier. She drank the rest of the liquid while watching Dedrick as he sat where he was, attempting to get some kind of control.

"Feel better?" she asked, her voice all sweet and soft.

Dedrick looked at her, his eyes still deep red. The expression almost brought her down to her knees again, but Jaclyn managed to stay upright. He also stood, and she said nothing. Once again, he was hard as stone, acting as if she hadn't just got him off. He headed toward her, appearing like the dark and dangerous predator she had been told he was.

Dedrick stopped a few inches from her body. His hands were clenched at his sides, his cock stood erect and proud, and his eyes roamed over her body with so much heat that Jaclyn felt her nipples become sensitive and rigid.

He grabbed her arms roughly, pulled her to him, and kissed her deep. Jaclyn moaned, squirmed for release. Once he did let her go, she wrapped her arms around his neck. Dedrick picked her up and she wrapped her legs around his waist. She gasped when he ripped her panties from her body and she squirmed in his arms when his lips trailed a heated path down her neck.

"Do you fuck as good as you taste?" she asked him.

"You're about to find out," Dedrick growled.

Dedrick pushed her up against the wall. He draped her legs over his strong arms, and not being the gentle type, Dedrick slammed her hot pussy onto his scorching cock.

Jaclyn never had the chance to give her body the small amount of time needed to get used to his size. Dedrick was thick and long and he stretched her to the point that she almost felt like a virgin again. He pounded into her like a man who was starving for release, and all she could do was hold on to whatever she could.

"Shit, yes." She moaned, bouncing on him and holding onto his shoulders. "Oh, god, yes!"

Her orgasm hit, and she screamed. In the past, Jaclyn always had some kind of warning that it was approaching, but this time, she had nothing. Her body contracted around his cock, which kept plunging in and out of her, and soon one orgasm turned into another, and then another.

Three orgasm was the max before Dedrick slammed into her one more time and came himself. His head went back, his black hair fanning out behind him. His hips jerked against her, and a deep moan rippled from his chest. Jaclyn felt his own release come out of him and into her.

Jaclyn wrapped her arms tightly around his neck, hugging herself to him. She loved the small aftershocks that gripped her. Just like she loved his male scent. She'd never experienced anything like it before. Dedrick was one of the best lovers she ever had. It was a shame that she was going to have to end things before they really got the chance to play.

Both were breathing fast and with some difficulty, but Dedrick broke the silence. His head was now resting on the wall, his hands still slightly hard inside her, and Jaclyn clinging to him.

"What the hell did we just do?" he asked, his voice starting to sound normal again. Sounding like the cool, collected guy that he was. Most of the time anyway.

Jaclyn rubbed her face against his neck. He really did smell damn good. "If you need me to explain what we just did, then you have problems." She laughed before taking a deep breath and letting it out slowly. "Want to do it again?"

Dedrick dropped her legs and moved away from her suddenly as if she was poison. "Do you have any idea what just fucking happened here?" he barked. "This isn't good!"

Jaclyn licked her lips and frowned at him. "That's funny." She worked at keeping her humorous face in place and not letting him see the pain she was starting to feel. Why was she feeling hurt when she knew this might be the reaction she was going to get if she messed around with him? "I thought you enjoyed yourself and knew perfectly well what you were doing." She grabbed her shoes, then stormed to the door. "My mistake. Won't happen again." Before he could get another word out, Jaclyn was out the door and slamming it in his face. She stood there with the door to her back, and the tears began to fall. "What did I just do?" she whispered to herself. "What the hell did I do?"

* * * *

Feeling like an ass, Dedrick stood looking at the closed door. He had known for the past couple of weeks that things were changing for him where Jaclyn Davis was concerned.

Tonight proved that his fears were dead-on—she was dangerous for him. Very fucking dangerous. And having sex with her only seemed to make things worse.

Dedrick believed that things with Jaclyn were quickly turning into a fatal attraction. Sure, she was hot, with a sweet ass to make any man's mouth water, but she was also human, and she was Sidney's best friend. Dedrick didn't want to make the biggest mistake of his life and break his no human rule, but he just did. In a matter of minutes, he just managed to screw himself into one nasty corner. He had sex with the one person he was trying like hell to avoid. If Sidney found out, she would fix him for life.

"Argh!" He picked up his half-full beer bottle and threw it hard against the wall. It shattered, spilling beer everywhere. "Why didn't I toss her pretty ass out the fucking door before this shit became so complicated?" he asked himself aloud.

"Sex always complicates things." Adrian stood in the doorway usual grin. "And I told you this was going to happen."

Dedrick walked over to where he'd tossed his briefs and yanked them on in anger while keeping his back to Adrian to hide some of his nudity. "What do you want?"

"I saw Jaclyn head over here." Adrian walked inside and closed the door. "Thought I'd come and help you out, but Skyler stopped me." Adrian glanced around the room and then at Dedrick. He sniffed the room. "But I guess nature took its course anyway."

"Save it, Adrian," Dedrick snapped out a warning. "I'm not in the mood."

"Dedrick." Adrian took a deep breath, let it out slowly, and placed his hands on his hips. "You just opened one hell of a can of worms here. Shit isn't going to be the same between the two of you now. Jaclyn has been sort of chasing after you since the first moment she laid eyes on you, remember? She's your damn mate, you dumb son of a bitch! You can't ignore it because Jaclyn happens to be a human." He took a deep breath. "If you don't come to terms with this, it's only going to bite you in the ass later."

"Get out, Adrian!" Dedrick became threatening. He didn't like others telling him all about the fuck-ups he'd made. He also didn't need a reminder where Jaclyn was concerned. "I don't need this shit right now."

"Did you mark her?"

Dedrick thought about it real quick and shook his head. He knew that he hadn't marked her, and it sort of bothered him.

"Well, I have to say I'm surprised." Dedrick frowned at Adrian. "Man, if you don't solve this little issue here, the shit is only going to boil over again, and you'll have a repeat of tonight. Full moon is at the end of the month. What are you going to do then?"

Dedrick ran his hands into his hair and groaned. "I don't know." He answered quietly. "I don't know why I even let her do..." He glanced at Adrian, who had one eyebrow up.

"Look just keep your mouth shut, okay? Let me try to figure this shit out. The family doesn't need to know."

Adrian nodded. "I won't say anything, but you're not going to keep it quiet for too long. Sidney can read Jaclyn like a book. She's going to know something's going on between the two of you."

"You just keep your mouth shut." Dedrick took a deep breath, letting it out slowly. "I'll figure something out."

"Okay." Adrian turned and went to the door. He opened it, but stopped and glanced back at Dedrick. "Keep your fingers crossed that

Stefan finds out, he is going to have your ass. Jaclyn is like another sister to him, in case you haven't noticed."

Chapter Three

Dedrick stayed away from the main house for the rest of the night. Early, around three in the morning, he woke from another dream about Jaclyn. Only this time, it wasn't a kissing dream, but a memory of them against the wall having the best sex ever. What had Dedrick waking in a cold sweat though was when he saw himself biting down on her neck, marking her as his own, scared that was what was going to happen if he didn't stay away from her. Jaclyn deserved better than him. She should marry a human and have human children. Not be mated to a beast like him who would probably never be able to give her children because of his DNA. He just didn't have enough human sperm to give her kids.

"Hey." Skyler peeked in with a smile, looked around the room, and then walked inside. "Mom wanted me to come and get you. She has a ton of leftovers and wants us all to help finish them off." Dedrick nodded and Skyler frowned. "Also, we're having a small family meeting." She rolled her eyes. "Bet Stefan is going to take Sidney away or something. You okay?"

Dedrick smiled, or tried. "I'm fine. Not sleeping too well."

Skyler chuckled. "Try being up at the house. The boys are keeping just about everyone up all night. They have their days and nights mixed up bad."

Dedrick grabbed his shoes to put them on, feeling his sister's eyes on him. "Skyler, you're staring."

"How'd you do that?"

"It's a gift." Standing, he sighed.

Together, they walked up to the main house. It was May already, and the temperature was hot. When he walked past the pool, he was reminded that he needed to fill it up, and he had promised his mother he would have it done a few weeks ago.

Dedrick hated to admit it, but he was a little nervous about going up to the house, nervous about facing Jaclyn after what they had done and wondering if by chance she might have said anything to Sidney. The sooner he faced Jaclyn and assured not only her but also himself that they could still be in the same room together, the better. He didn't want her thinking that just because they had sex, they couldn't be civil.

Leftovers were the main meal, as Skyler said it would be. When Dedrick walked into the dining room, the family was already seated and eating. Stefan and Sidney each had a sleeping baby in their arms. Jaclyn was talking to Natasha and Adrian just seemed to be relaxing.

took his seat.

"Good, you're here," Natasha said.

Jaclyn stopped talking and glanced at him. He felt his heart thump, and he waited for her to say something, but she didn't. She smiled at something that Skyler said, and it hit him that she had never really smiled at him before. For some unknown reason, that and the fact that she didn't pay much attention to him bothered him more than if she would have just started her usual shit.

"Stefan wants to take Sidney on a quick honeymoon," Natasha said. "And I'm having the pool house remodeled." She looked at Skyler. "I want you two to move in."

"Mom!" Skyler gasped.

"You two need some privacy." Natasha smiled. "Jaclyn has also agreed to stay on longer to give me a hand with the boys while Stefan and Sidney are gone."

He frowned at Jaclyn, but she didn't glance back at him. "Thought you were in a hurry to leave again?"

"I changed my mind." She stared him directly in the eye.

Dedrick forced his own eyes away. He kept telling himself that if he looked at her for too long, then everyone was going to suspect something, so he diverted his attention to Adrian. "What's on your mind?"

Adrian shook his head. "Nothing."

"I thought you wanted to go skiing?" Skyler said.

Dedrick locked eyes with Adrian. "I do." Adrian said. "But we might have to wait until your brother comes back first."

"Oh, come on," Natasha huffed. "There is no reason why you both can't take your wives on a trip. I think Dedrick, Jaclyn, and I can handle things around the house just fine."

Dedrick tore his eyes from Adrian to smile at his mother. "Sure we can." He gave a quick glance at Jaclyn.

Oh, he could feel it. She was about to blow, and Dedrick desperately wanted to get his mother and Sidney for sure out of the room before she did so. His gut was screaming that Jaclyn was about to say or do something.

"See." Natasha shifted her eyes from Adrian to Stefan. "Everything is under control. And I swear if I could handle Stefan and Dedrick, I'm sure I can handle the twins."

"Why don't we flip for it?" Stefan stated. "I just have a strange feeling that something might happen if both Adrian and I are gone at the same time." He pulled out a quarter from his pocket. "How about go."

Adrian grinned, then sat up in his chair quickly. "Okay, but I want heads."

Dedrick couldn't believe this. "You two act like I can't be trusted," he grumbled.

"Your temperament leaves much to be desired," Jaclyn said at him.

He raised one eyebrow toward her, but kept his mouth shut. Dedrick wasn't going to start a fight with her.

"Shit," Stefan said under his breath.

"Hah!" Adrian clapped his hands together. "Baby, pack the warm blanket, 'cause we're going skiing."

"You just got lucky." Stefan pointed his finger at Adrian.

"Well, I think we need to get these two in bed," Sidney said to Stefan. Before she stood up, she looked at Jaclyn. "And don't start it again."

"Here, give me one," Natasha said to Stefan. "I'll help her put the boys down. You finish your supper."

Dedrick watched his mother leave the room with one of the babies. Since their birth, the house had definitely not been quiet.

"Don't start what?" Dedrick looked around the room for someone to answer the question.

"Oh, I'm not supposed to fight with you." Jaclyn sneered. "I think she thinks it will ruffle those delicate feathers of yours.

"And don't forget about Sidney twisting your arm on the moving in issue." Stefan chuckled.

Jaclyn shook her fork at him. "She hasn't won anything yet."

"You're still here," Stefan teased. "And if memory serves me—" He glanced up at the ceiling as if he was thinking or recalling something—"you told her that if she could pin you down, then you would."

"She wouldn't have gotten a hold of me if you hadn't bolted the damn door," she said with as little emotion as she could. "You are so pussy-whipped."

"And proud of it." Stefan smiled brightly, showing his teeth before taking a bite out of an apple.

"And speaking of pussy-whipped. Dedrick!" Jaclyn finally gave her full attention to him and he felt his gut drop. The expression she gave him was one that spoke of nothing but trouble. "You seem different. Not so hard." She cocked her head to one side, and her thick hair fell over her shoulder. To him, she seemed like a dark angel sent from hell to torture him to death. "Why is that?"

"You know, she has a point," Stefan remarked, wiping his mouth with the napkin. "You do seem different. More relaxed."

"Jaclyn..." Dedrick tried to send out a warning with his voice, but she either didn't get it or ignored it.

"Almost has that, I-got-laid look." Jaclyn grinned at Stefan before turning the expression on him. "Did you?"

Adrian spit his drink out and coughed. Dedrick on the other hand met her challenging eyes with one of his own. An eyebrow went up, and he grinned. "Maybe I did. Jealous?"

"Oh, shit," Adrian mumbled.

"I think I'm going to help Mom," Skyler said, pushing away from the table and dashing from the room before more was said.

Jaclyn smiled. "Not on your life." She also pushed away from the table. She acted as if she didn't give a damn. "Well, she must have been damn good to make you look..." She cocked her head to the other side, her eyes roaming over him. "...satisfied...almost normal."

Dedrick's frown turned into a grin. He couldn't help it. Her challenges made him feel something he hadn't felt in many years—alive. "You know, I also see something in you. Did you get laid too?"

This time it was Stefan who spit out his drink and coughed. Adrian groaned.

Jaclyn grinned, but her eyes told of something else. Jaclyn was pissed—at him. "Wouldn't you like to know?" She tossed her napkin on the table and strolled over to him. "But if I did, then he has already slipped my mind. What does that tell you?" She stopped next to him and leaned down so only he could hear. "No one knows and never will. A mistake that until this moment was forgotten." She straightened up and smiled at Stefan and Adrian. "'Night, boys."

Dedrick sat there staring straight ahead with a slight grin on his face, while biting the inside of his lip. A mistake? Was it really? He glanced at Adrian, frowned, and thought about what Adrian had said. Was she really his?

"What the hell was that?" Stefan asked.

"Don't ask," Adrian answered. His eyes met Dedrick dead on. "Trust me. You don't want to know."

* * * *

"You going out?" Sidney walked into Jaclyn's room just as Jaclyn left the bathroom, her head down, as she tied a thick belt around her waist.

Jaclyn was a petite five-foot-three with long, black hair that reached her waistline, with sparkling blue eyes, and sensual lips. More than once, Sidney wished that she looked like her and possessed her confidence. Jaclyn had narrow hips that rounded out to well-formed legs, which looked good in everything. She wasn't a skinny girl, but she was in damn good shape and still had a flat stomach.

"Yeah," Jaclyn answered. "I need a drink or two."

"I was hoping that you would stay and watch a movie with us." Sidney hated this. Whenever something was wrong, Jaclyn had to leave. Sure, she was staying at the house with them, but she was still leaving, going to the bars and clubs until after closing.

"Not tonight," Jaclyn said. Sidney watched her sit on the bed and pull her cowboy boots on her feet. She was dressed in her usual short skirt, this one cotton, and a tight tank top that showed a good amount of her stomach. Even if it was May and hot, that was no excuse for her to go out dressed like a tramp, Sidney thought.

"Do you have to wear that?" Sidney snorted. "Makes you look..." She couldn't finish the thought.

"Easy?" Jaclyn glanced up at her.

"That's not funny." Sidney couldn't help herself and started to cry. The postpartum depression was killing her. She couldn't sleep with Stefan and couldn't deal with the boys, and to add more icing to her cake, Jacy was running from something and wouldn't talk to her about it.

"Hey!" Jaclyn quickly stood and went to her. She hugged Sidney and rubbed her back. "Damn it, don't start the crying again."

"Why can't you stay in with us?" Sidney whined.

"I'm right here!" Jaclyn answered, stepping back and brushing some of the tears away. "You need to have some time with Stefan, alone. Like now!" She chuckled. "I want you to snuggle up with that hot man of yours and relax without me or anyone else around."

"But I don't want you to go." Sidney sighed. "You're always going out and coming back toasted."

"Hot date tonight?" Dedrick asked as he roamed his eyes over her body while leaning against the doorframe.

Jaclyn took a deep breath and turned to him. Aggravation was written all over her face and directed right at him. Sidney quickly picked up that something was going on between the two of them. "None of your damn business." She turned back to Sidney. "I've got to go."

"True," he continued, acting as if she hadn't said anything. "Going to wear that?"

Jaclyn grabbed her keys from the nightstand and walked up to him. "Don't start with me."

Sidney groaned and followed Jaclyn out and down the stairs. She didn't understand why Dedrick was there or following, but her gut was screaming that he was the reason Jaclyn was going out.

"Better get your price down before you go out the door. Don't want to confuse the guys and all," Dedrick said.

"Dedrick!" Sidney yelled. "You're not helping."

"Fuck you, Dedrick!" Jaclyn snapped.

"For how much?" he snapped back.

Sidney could hear the controlled anger in his voice. She remembered Stefan sounding the same way when she first came here.

Jaclyn stopped at the bottom of the stairs, turned toward Dedrick, her eyes narrowing on him. She walked back up the steps, put her hand on his chest, and pushed him but he didn't move. "Don't go there. I don't belong to you or anyone, so you don't get to tell me what the hell I can or can't do or how to dress." She poked him in the chest. "So piss off." She kneed him in the gut hard enough to cause Dedrick to grunt and lose his breath. "Don't wait up," she said to Sidney, slamming the door closed.

"Jaclyn!" Sidney yelled. She turned on Dedrick, and, with disbelief in her voice, said, "What the hell is wrong with you?"

Dedrick rubbed his gut. "Thank God she didn't go lower." He took a deep breath and let it out slowly. "Could have caused some damage."

"Dedrick!" she cried, feeling a fresh wave of tears threatening to fall.

"Oh, don't worry about it." He groaned while pushing up from the stairs. "She'll have a few drinks, cool off and come back."

"Argh!" Sidney followed him through Natasha's sitting room back to the family room. "Dedrick, I'm so damn tired of the tension between you two." She grabbed his arm, stopped him, and turned him so he was facing her. "What the hell is going on? Ever since the party you two have been acting very strange."

Sidney studied him, but Dedrick was good. If he were hiding something, then he was hiding it perfectly. "I don't understand this," she went on. "You two seem to be at each other's throats worse than ever. Why can't you get along with her?"

Dedrick tapped a finger on his lip, pretending he was thinking hard. "Because she acts like a bitch most of the time?" He shrugged. He started laughing when Sidney tried to hit him. "I'm kidding! I swear, I'm kidding!"

told Sidney, with no interest in his voice, as he walked into the room with a movie in his hand. "Mom will want an explanation."

"I'm not joking, Dedrick." She managed to land one hard blow to the back of his head before he backed away. "This shit between the two of you needs to stop."

"There's nothing between us." Dedrick tried to act and sound innocent. It didn't work. Sidney glared, moving to sit beside Stefan on the loveseat. She knew enough about Dedrick to know that he was hiding something.

"There's something going on." Sidney huffed. "And I'm going to figure it out."

"What's the deal with her mother?" Stefan asked as he put the movie in the player.

"I don't know." Sidney sighed. "Her mother remembers she has a daughter when she needs something."

"So who paid for her college?" Stefan asked. When Sidney frowned, he shrugged and went on. "I looked into her background when I was…um…you know, looking for the best way to convince you to come home with me."

"Convinced with a drug infused cocktail." Dedrick smirked.

"Don't you have some place to be?" Stefan frowned at Dedrick and his lips thinned out which told Sidney he didn't want to be reminded about how he brought her home.

"I don't know. Scholarship, I think." Sidney sighed. "The story she told me was that she was a straight-A student in high school and graduated early, started college, and that's where I met up with her. She didn't go home on the holidays, so I took her home with me until we started to do our own thing. She's very smart," Sidney went on, looking at Dedrick. "She has a degree in business and has had her hand in the stock market from time to time. I know she got some money from that, and that has to be what she's been living on."

"Well, that would explain how she bounces from place to place," Stefan said.

"Right, and I don't want her bouncing out the door again," Sidney stated, giving Dedrick a glare. "So you need to figure out a way to get along with her, or the next time she leaves, I may never see her again."

"Come on, Sid." Dedrick sighed, rubbing his face. "She isn't running because she can. Your friend is running because she's scared of something."

The twins started crying, and Stefan dropped his head back on the sofa. "Not again."

two need some time alone."

Dedrick left, but Sidney couldn't shake the feeling like there was a lot more going on than what she saw. "Something's going on."

Stefan wrapped his arm around her shoulders and pulled her closer. "They're just at each other again. Don't worry about it so much."

"You didn't see them on the stairs." Sidney sighed, putting her head on his chest. "She had a look like she could kill him."

"Everybody wants to kill Dedrick at one time or another," Stefan said. "It's nothing new. He probably just said something that pissed her off. She'll cool off and go back to drooling and giving him shit."

Sidney sat there thinking about that. Maybe Dedrick did say something that upset Jaclyn. It wouldn't be the first time he had her seeing red. Hell, the last time he picked her up from the airport was definitely the last time, and still Sidney hadn't gotten the entire story of what happened. All she got was that Dedrick made it very clear to Jaclyn he didn't mess around with humans. Period!

"Stefan, do you think it is?" Sidney sat up and turned to face him. "Do you think she tried to proposition him, and he turned her down?"

Stefan shrugged. "Could be. She wouldn't be the first one he turned down."

Sidney sat back and rested against him. "It would certainly explain a lot."

* * * *

Dedrick spent an hour with the twins, feeding and putting them back to bed. At one in the morning, he was in his room, where he stripped down to nothing and slid between the cool sheets. May was turning out to be one hell of a hot month and extra brutal for shifters. Sure, they had central air, but it didn't do much to cool down an overheated body, and right now, Dedrick's was steaming. He was hot and horny. Not a good combination.

Finally, he slept deeply, hot, but relaxed with the sheet barely covering his body. In fact, he had moved so much that the sheet had slipped between his legs, hiding his cock but that was all. It all came crashing to an abrupt end when he felt ice-cold water dumped on his face and poured down his bare chest.

"Son of a bitch!" Dedrick cried out, sitting up fast. He shook his head causing water to go everywhere on his bed. He looked up and saw Jaclyn standing before him with a furious expression on her face. "What the hell was that for?"

"Be a prick again, and I'm going to superglue your nuts to your leg." Jaclyn hit him hard in the chest. "You keep acting like this, and something happened between us, and your little damn secret goes right out the door."

"I think I liked my nuts in your mouth better," he grumbled, wiping the water from his chest and shaking his head again. "And she isn't going to find out shit."

Jaclyn made a move to hit him again, but Dedrick was ready for it. He grabbed hold of her around the waist and body slammed her down on the bed. He covered her body with his, pinning her wrists over her head.

"Finished yet?" He grunted, fighting to hold her down. Dedrick hated to admit it, but having her under him felt pretty damn good.

"Get the fuck off me!" she said through gritted teeth.

Dedrick continued to hold her arms over her head and just looked down at her. His body was only half over her. One leg was bent between her legs, and his hip rested on one of her legs. The sheet kept his cock from touching her skin. With her dressed in her skirt, the only thing separating him from paradise was a thin pair of panties that could be ripped off with no problem.

He lowered his head down to hers, his lips mere inches from touching and eyes locked to hers. "I don't want to."

"Dedrick, you shouldn't be . . ."

He didn't let her finish her statement. He swooped down and claimed her lips, kissed her deep, thrusting his tongue in. She tasted like warm honey—sweet honey, which could quickly turn into a drug to his senses if he wasn't careful. He moaned into her mouth when he felt her relax under him. Dedrick let go of her wrists, moved his right hand down the side of her body, and hooked, first one leg, then the other, over his waist. Then he moved his hand to her ass and hugged her closer.

He was on fire, yet knowing he was playing a dangerous game. But damn if she didn't taste good. He moved the hand on her ass under her skirt and bunched up her panties with the intent to rip them off, and would have if his other hand hadn't touched the cool water on the bed when he moved to better position himself between her legs. The small touch of water was enough to bring his senses back together and remind him he was about to make a mistake again. Sex with Jaclyn just wasn't an option for him.

With a growl, Dedrick pushed himself away from Jaclyn and off the bed. He grabbed the sheet quickly and wrapped it around his waist, covering his nakedness. "Shit. You're right. We shouldn't do this." He hung his head and looked around the room, anywhere he could besides her.

When he glanced up, she was scooting off the bed. Dedrick thought he saw tears in her eyes, but nothing fell. However, the sadness he saw in her eyes hurt him as well.

"Jaclyn . . ."

She raised her hand, stopping him from saying anything else. "Don't. I get it, I really do." He watched her walk to the door and open it. "'Night, Dedrick," she said softly before closing the door behind her.

"Son of a bitch." He sighed, running a hand in his hair. "What now?"

* * * *

"Come on, Sid said I could borrow it." Jaclyn was in the kitchen with Stefan when Dedrick walked in. Neither saw him, which was good. He wasn't ready yet to face her after the kiss thing.

"Sidney might have said you could, but it wasn't cleared with me." Stefan grinned. "How do I know that you won't run away with my car?"

Dedrick chuckled and walked in, heading right for the coffee. "I wouldn't trust her." he said with his back to them both. "She might try to head for Mexico."

"Piss off, Dedrick," Jaclyn said. "Come on, Stefan. I have a meeting."

"Where's Sid, by the way?" Dedrick asked, taking a sip from his cup.

"In the shower," Stefan answered. "We have to take the boys to their three-month check-up. Also, Sidney needs to go in and see the doctor about her depression."

"Stefan." Jaclyn tapped her foot on the floor and held out her hand.

"If I let you have the car, then I can't take Sid and the boys in," Stefan said.

Adrian walked into the kitchen yawning. "Morning."

"Morning?" Dedrick snorted. "It's almost noon, you shit."

"I know," Adrian remarked, heading for the coffee as well. "Sky just woke me up and told me to pack. We leave in a couple hours."

"I thought you were leaving next week," Stefan said.

"She changed her mind." Adrian smiled.

"Hello!" Jaclyn waved her hands in the air and got all three of their attention. "I need a damn car."

"Don't look at me, babe," Adrian said. "I'm heading out of town in a few."

"I can't, Jaclyn," Stefan also said.

Natasha came in with her purse under her arm.

Jaclyn smiled. "Nothing. I'm going to call a cab."

"Oh, don't do that." Natasha shook her head. "Dedrick, you take her where she needs to go."

Dedrick almost choked on his coffee. "Excuse me? Why can't you?"

"I'm going to the store," Natasha answered. "You three have eaten everything in the house. And if Jaclyn has an appointment, she might be late in getting there with me or I could be late picking her up." She crossed her arms over her chest. "Besides, you don't have anything going on today. You can do it."

Dedrick didn't like the expression his mother gave him. She had a don't-defy-me look with an eyebrow raised, and Dedrick knew that he couldn't tell his mother no without giving her a damn good reason for it.

"Fine," he growled, banging his cup down on the counter. "I'll get my damn keys."

"Thank you." Natasha smiled. "See, dear, everything's all worked out."

Dedrick waited in the hallway for Jaclyn as she went up to change. Stefan and Sidney had already left with the boys for their doctor's appointment. Natasha took off right after he agreed to take Jaclyn, and Adrian and Skyler were up packing for their trip.

As he waited for her, Dedrick thought about the boys. They were three months old, but the way they were growing and acting, Dedrick could tell they were a major handful. He would also put a large amount of money that they would soon be walking before the normal age since they were half shifter.

Most shifter children grow faster in their first five years of life than human children do. Their DNA evolved to require this rapid growth cycle for the sole purpose of the survival of the race. The motto of the shifters became Only the Strong Survive. The surviving males were responsible for providing for their families. Over the years, it had been discovered the shifter children had a strong sense of awareness. They could sense everything going on around them and understand what it all meant. This sixth sense was so highly developed the children were able to save themselves from danger because they "knew" it was going to happen before it did. Consequently, this meant more children were surviving to adulthood. Dedrick's nephews were using this sixth sense now. They had the shifter DNA for rapid growth.

Dedrick was about to go up and see what was taking her so long stairs dressed in jeans and a light business jacket with her long hair French braided down the middle of her back.

"About time," he grumbled. "Thought you were on a time schedule."

"Let's just get this over with." She jerked the front door open.

"Fine by me."

Dedrick followed her, reached around to open her door, then to the other side, getting into the car without saying anything further. She did tell him it was Starbucks where she needed to go, and he answered with a nod. As he drove, he kept thinking about the shit going on between the two of them during the past few weeks.

First, she kissed him, and then he had sex with her, then back to the kissing. Dedrick didn't understand what the hell was going on with him. It was dangerous for him to be messing around with a human, especially Jaclyn Davis. With his history with humans as lovers, he knew the only thing that could come out of this was pain for her and loneliness for him. He was just too much of an animal for her.

Sure Stefan got lucky and mated with a human, but his brother was different. Stefan wasn't as hard as Dedrick or as dark. He didn't feel the lingering danger that Dedrick felt each day or fought each month. If he didn't find his mate, then Dedrick feared he was going to have to leave his family in order to protect them.

The beast lingering inside was fast becoming deadly, and Dedrick didn't know how much longer he was going to be able to control it. Once that control slipped, there was no going back for a shifter. They were like rabid dogs needing to be put down. That was why it was so important for males to find their mates. Whoever would be able to give his animal side what it needed and help keep him in control. And he was damn sure that someone wasn't Jaclyn.

He drove up to the coffee shop and parked. "Can I go in and get a cup, or does the lapdog have to stay out in the car?"

"Give it a rest," she snapped, getting out of the car.

Dedrick followed her inside and went over to the counter. After ordering a coffee and a pastry, he sat down at a table. He watched as Jaclyn sat down at a table, across the room, where a man in a business suit was waiting. Just watching her talk to this guy caused Dedrick to growl low, then curse himself for doing it. Why did he give a damn?

Once again, he had to remind himself that she was human. He was shifter. The two weren't ever going to mix. Then, the little voice in his head reminded him that they already had. They'd had sex, and even though Dedrick hated the idea, not the act itself he wanted to do it wrapped around him, to hear her moans, to smell her desire. He hungered for her taste, and it worried him with the coming full moon what might happen. Dedrick didn't trust himself. Having sex with her that one time had started something that he wasn't ready for or wanted to face. Hell, it sure wasn't going to be safe for her if she was in the house this month during his heat.

Twenty minutes later, Jaclyn and that man were still talking. From where he was sitting, the meeting didn't appear to be going well. They continued to drink coffee. After an hour, the meeting broke up, and Jaclyn was pissed. Dedrick stayed put, waiting for her to come to him. When she didn't, he stood up and walked over to her.

"Meeting didn't go well?" he asked, taking the seat the man had vacated.

"Don't worry about it." She pushed from the table and stood up. "Can we go?"

Dedrick held his cup up. "Not finished with my drink." She sighed and sat back down, giving him a dirty look. He frowned. "Are you pissed at me?"

"What do you think?" She crossed her arms over her chest and then rubbed her forehead as if she had a headache. "Look, Dedrick. This game you're playing, you need to tell me the rules here, or we're just going to keep going round and round in circles."

"You're a temptation I don't need," he stated in a gruff voice. "Nothing good can come from us messing around together."

Jaclyn sat back in her chair. "Temptation is all around, Dedrick. Learn to deal with it, I have." She stood up. "But don't worry. Before you know it, I'll be gone again and your life can go back to that boring routine you love so much." She moved around the back of the chair and pushed it in. "I have some shopping to do. I'll catch a cab back to the house. Make sure and tell Sid I'll be home by dinner."

* * * *

Boring routine. That was what kept going over and over in Dedrick's head during dinner. Sidney was telling Jaclyn what the doctor had said about the boys. Even though the boys were three months old, their minds were developing fast, which meant they were equivalent to a nine-month-old human baby. Their bodies would soon be catching up. Sidney was busy explaining to everyone how the boys should be trying to crawl by next month and that by age eight months they could be walking.

Jaclyn went with Sidney to tuck the boys in for the night. Not even once, since she came home from her shopping, had she acknowledged

Skyler had already left to go skiing when he returned home and Natasha had just pulled in with her car full of food.

Stefan was cleaning the kitchen up while Dedrick sat at the table. He was busy thinking about everything Jaclyn had said earlier. How he felt about it had his fingers drumming on the table. The thought of her leaving again for a long time didn't sit well with him. He wasn't sure how he felt about what was coming to his mind either. Was Adrian right? Could she be his?

"You okay?" Stefan asked.

Dedrick looked up at his brother and frowned. "Yeah, why?"

Stefan pulled out two beers from the fridge and handed one to him. "You've been acting funny."

Dedrick twisted the cap off and took a deep drink before he turned to Stefan. How could he tell him what he was thinking about was Jaclyn? How he couldn't get the sex they'd shared off his mind. Dedrick knew that if Stefan found out about the two of them, the shit was going to hit the fan.

Dedrick sighed. "Guess I'm just dreading another heat alone."

"So what're you going to do?"

Dedrick brought the bottle up to his lips and stopped. "No clue," he said before taking a drink.

"Maybe you should go to a Gathering," Stefan tossed back at him. "Might get lucky and find your mate there."

"Why can't mine land in my lap like Sidney did for you?" Dedrick groaned.

Stefan cracked a short laugh. "She didn't land in my lap. I landed in hers."

"Same thing." Dedrick shrugged.

"Dedrick, I don't mean to sound cynical here, but you haven't opened the doors for anyone to land in your lap." Stefan frowned, scratching his chin. "You have been so damn scared your mate is going to be a human that you have practically shut the world out."

"And what do I do if she does end up being human?" Dedrick glanced over at his brother. "I don't want to hurt another woman."

"Shit." Stefan mumbled the word and took another drink. "You tried to fuck that human hours before your heat. That's why you almost hurt her. I think if your mate was there, human or not, she would be able to handle what you need to release."

"So how did you know Sidney was the one for you?"

Stefan smiled with a faraway expression on his face while he was reliving the past. His blue eyes glazed over. "I felt alive for the first from his lips, almost in a dreamlike way. "Never felt that before. It was a mixture of being at peace and raging inside."

Dedrick understood all too well that raging inside. He received his first taste of the peace Stefan was referring to the night in the pool house with Jaclyn. Dedrick desperately wanted it again but was too damn scared to take the step. He couldn't afford to be wrong about Jaclyn.

"Look, Dedrick." Stefan placed his bottle on the table and leaned forward. "You need to go out more. That's what it all comes down to. It's the only way you're going to find your mate." Stefan stood up and left Dedrick sitting at the table.

Dedrick took another beer from the fridge. He left the kitchen to go up to his room. He stopped when he saw Jaclyn coming down the stairs in her short skirt and tight top.

"Where the hell are you going?" he demanded. He damned himself for the way he sounded when he asked that question. He sounded angry almost like she was his and he had the right to know where she was going all the time.

She stopped when she opened the door and looked at him. "Out."

"You went out last night," he stated.

"Yes, and I didn't find what I was looking for." She tossed her long hair over her shoulder. "Tonight I'm hoping to change my luck."

Dedrick gritted his teeth together so tightly it caused his jaw to ache. He hated how the thought of another man touching her pissed him off.

"Jaclyn," he warned but didn't get to finish his speech because she was out the door. "Damn it!" he growled.

Chapter Four

Stefan walked into the club with a sigh at three thirty in the morning, thanks to a call from the bartender and Sydney's laments. Sidney was the only one to get him out this late at night to pick Jaclyn up in God only knew what kind of state. He was guessing very drunk and wasn't disappointed when he saw her.

She was sitting on a stool at the bar, swaying to the music with many beer bottles, and shot glasses in front of her. He headed her way, thinking to himself, yep she's toasted. Before he sat down next to her or let her know he was there, Stefan got the attention of the bartender and gave him the cut off sign for Jaclyn.

"Having a good time?" Stefan asked, sliding onto the stool, staring at her to see her reaction.

"Stefan!" Jaclyn cried out, smiling and turning in her seat, to face him. "I'm having a kick-ass time. Want to join me?"

She looked very drunk, but only had a slight slur to her words. Despite her smile, she appeared to be hurt about something. He grinned. "Don't think so."

"Too bad." She turned back taking a drink from her beer. "I'm waiting for Mister Right to come along and rock my world, but the bastard hasn't showed up yet."

"Come on, Jacy." He tugged on her arm. "Let's get you home."

"Naw!" She pulled her arm from his hand. "I'm not done yet."

Stefan took a deep breath and let it out real slow. "So what's the special occasion then?"

"It helps me forget." She took her last shot and hissed. "And helps take the edge off."

"What are you trying to forget?" She didn't look at him. Raising a red flag for Stefan couldn't have made him more curious. What was she trying to forget? Sidney must not know about it or Jacy would be sharing what her problem was.

"Do you know that I don't have a home?" She grinned, keeping her eyes on her beer bottle. "I think I'm starting to want what Sidney has, but damn if I know how to go about getting it." She took a drink. "There's a lot of things I want but can't have." She chuckled then. "Guess that's life." She turned to him. "I have a step-brother. Did you know that?" Stefan shook his head. "No one knows. He's a fucking loser like my mother and his father, and his parole is coming up again." She finished the drink in front of her, then slammed the glass down on the bar. "Son-of-a-bitch lawyer of his wants me to help him get out." She rubbed her face. "I need to get laid, Stefan."

He coughed. "Well, dating might help."

She laughed then. "I've been trying that, but damn if it ain't helping either." Smiling back at her, Stefan watched while she finished off the last of her beer and hiccupped. "You know. I think I might be a little drunk."

"And you will feel it in the morning." He chuckled.

Jaclyn snorted. "Then I'll just start over to dull that pain."

"Come on." Stefan got down from the stool and helped Jaclyn do the same. He swung her arm over his shoulder and, taking most of her weight, found her lighter than he expected. "Let's get you home to sleep it off."

"I told you," she slurred. "I don't have a home."

"Well, for now, you have a permanent room in *my* home," he told her. "How's that? And you can even call it your home if you want."

They made it to the door when she stopped. "Stefan, I'm going to tell you something that's going to have you in so much shock, but I have to say it to someone, you know? And I don't think Sidney would like it." She stood in front of him, put both hands on his chest, rubbed his shirt collar, and swayed on her feet. "And please don't judge me, okay? I get enough of that in my life."

"I promise." He smiled, trying to get her out the door.

"I fucked your brother." That got Stefan to stop dead in his tracks and stare at her. "And I loved it," she said with a frown. "I loved it, loved how protected I felt in his arms, the power in his body, all of it." She sighed. "And I want to do it all over again, but I think he hates me." Her voice broke like she might start to cry, and she seemed lost and sad. "He hates me because I'm human." She patted his shoulders, her eyes dropping. "And you know what one of the worst things is? I still want to do it again." She looked confused when she glanced at him. "How come he can't be more like you and like humans? I can treat him real good you know. Do all those wild things in bed and…and…"

"Jaclyn . . ." Stefan lowered his voice and tried to get her to focus for a few seconds so he could get her out of the bar. He really didn't want to hear all the details of her having sex with his brother.

"I have been trying to date other guys, Stefan." She swayed a little on her feet, which caused him to have to hold her up. "I have even tried to have sex with others, but it's not there." She shrugged. "I want him." Her smile was faint, and the pain clear in her eyes. "You were right. I should never have messed with him, but I did. And now you know why

I can't stay at your home any longer. I need to leave before it's too late."

Stefan wasn't sure what to say, or what to do, for that matter, but his gut was screaming that it might be too late already. "Let's work on that later, okay? Right now, if I don't get you home, Sidney is going to have my ass."

Jaclyn smiled. "She loves you, and that's nice. She needs to be loved."

Stefan agreed with her all the way to his car. Once he had her in, he rubbed his face and took a deep breath. Jaclyn and Dedrick had messed around. Holy shit! That explained so much of the tension right now, but why in the hell hadn't he seen it? It was right in front of him with the quick glances Dedrick gave her. *Son of a bitch!*

By the time they reached home, Jaclyn had passed out. Stefan had to carry her into the house and was not surprised now to find Dedrick waiting with Sidney on the stairs. He gave Dedrick a dirty look and kept his mouth shut.

"What happened?" Sidney cried.

"She just passed out," Stefan answered. "She was pretty toasted when I got there and in a confessing mood." He shot another dirty look at Dedrick when he passed him to take the stairs two at a time.

"Damn." Sidney sighed. "She hasn't gotten this drunk in years, or passed out from it."

Stefan didn't say anything further, just headed to the guest room Jaclyn was using for the time being. He left her on the bed for Sidney to undress and tuck in. Stefan grabbed his brother's arm and dragged him out of the room to his own. He shoved Dedrick in and slammed the door.

"You better have a good damn reason for dragging me in here like *I* was the little brother," Dedrick barked.

Stefan ran a hand through his hair and placed the other on his waist. "You want to tell me what the fuck is going on between you and Jaclyn?" he demanded, growling, "And no bullshit either."

"Nothing," Dedrick said. He sounded calm, almost too damn calm.

Stefan stared hard at his brother, and for once, Dedrick seemed to squirm under his eyes. "Bullshit."

"Stefan..."

"I want the fucking truth before my wife comes in here," Stefan snapped. "Did you have sex with Jaclyn?"

Dedrick crossed his arms over his chest and gave Stefan a scornful look. Normally, when Dedrick glared at him like this, he would have

"Yes," he answered through his teeth.

"Son of a bitch," he mumbled with a defeated shake of his head. "How could you do that?"

"It's not what you think," Dedrick said again.

"Oh, you don't know what I think." Stefan chuckled, pacing the room.

"She came to me in the pool house the night of the party." That got Stefan to stop his pacing and glare at him. He opened his mouth to go on, but Stefan stopped him again.

"You had sex with her the night of the party!" Stefan's voice hitched.

"Stefan, will you listen to me?" Dedrick barked. "It happened. *I* didn't plan it."

"Of course not." He raised his hands into the air before stuffing them in his pockets. "But did you learn from Adrian what happens when you screw around? Hell no!"

"Fuck." Dedrick groaned. "I didn't screw around. What do you want me to say?"

"You don't say anything." Stefan pointed his finger at his brother. He was pissed. "Jaclyn is about ready to bolt again. Did you know that? Because I can see it tonight in her eyes and in the way she talks. She wanted you! For Christ sakes, Dedrick." He paced again twice before stopping and pointing his finger at Dedrick once more. "This time *you* are going to be the one to keep her here. You started this god damn mess, and you better clean the shit up!"

"Oh, come on, Stefan," Dedrick groaned. "We can't stand being in the same room together. You saw that."

"Pull that shit on someone else." Stefan smirked. "I've seen how she's been around you." He shook his head, frowning at Dedrick. "Why the hell do you think she tries to pick a fight?" Stefan snapped. "Sidney wants her to stay. Jaclyn needs a home. Mom has agreed to having her move in with us permanently, and you pull this shit!" He raised his arms up in the air. "Un-fucking-believable! You had better find a damn way to keep her here."

Dedrick lowered his eyes and rubbed his jaw. "Stefan..." he growled.

"No!" Stefan yelled. "We want her here. You think of something to keep her here!" Stefan saw him thinking, and the way Stefan was feeling right now, he didn't give a damn what his brother did if it kept Jaclyn here.

"I don't have time for this shit." Dedrick's voice lowered, and his coming, and you want me to think up something to make her stay when I'm trying like hell to *keep* away from her!"

"Yes, I do!" Stefan snapped back. "I know she wants you. She told me herself." Dedrick frowned, and his mouth opened. "And you're just going to have to deal with it."

"I can't believe I'm having this conversation with you," Dedrick grumbled.

"Would you prefer Mom or Adrian?" Dedrick's eyes narrowed on Stefan as he started to pace the room. With that look, Stefan knew. "Don't tell me that Adrian knew and I didn't?" Again, he only glared at Stefan. "Son of a bitch! Adrian knew, and I didn't!"

"He walked in after," Dedrick mumbled.

"What the hell is going on around here?"

"What in the world is all the yelling about?" Natasha walked into the bedroom, frowning at both of them. "Are you two trying to wake the boys up?"

"You fix this," Stefan snarled.

"What's wrong?" Natasha asked.

"Nothing, Mother." Dedrick looked at Stefan, not their mother. "I was just going to bed." He turned and headed to the door, but stopped at Stefan's voice.

"Dedrick . . ." Stefan warned.

"Don't push me, Stefan." He glanced over his shoulder at Stefan. "You won't like how it ends. I promise you." Before saying another word, Dedrick was out the door.

"You want to tell me what's going on?" Natasha asked.

"Trust me, you don't want to know." Stefan sighed.

* * * *

"You really outdid yourself this time." Sidney stood outside the bathroom as Jaclyn threw her guts up in the toilet.

"I don't need the lecture, Sid." Jaclyn moaned, waiting for her stomach to settle. It didn't, and over she went again.

"You going to tell me what's going on?"

Jaclyn finished a third round of bowing to the porcelain god, flushed the toilet, and stood up to brush her teeth. Once she was finished, she splashed some cold water on her face and opened the bathroom door. "There's nothing going on."

"Jacy, you haven't drunk like this since we were in school, and it was after that guy dumped you."

Jaclyn dropped face-down on the bed, her face in the pillow. She felt like shit. Her sides hurt from throwing up, her stomach was still to pound. Yep, she was going to have one hell of a hangover in the morning. But the drinking did help. She was able to dull the rejection from Dedrick with a few good shots of tequila, or maybe it was a whole bottle. She couldn't remember.

"Jaclyn." Sidney turned her over in the bed and Jaclyn sighed.

"Sidney, I just drank too much." She covered her eyes with her arm. "And now I need to sleep it off."

"Okay," Sidney said. "I'm here when you're ready to talk."

Jaclyn stayed where she was, acting like she was falling asleep. The moment the lights went out and the door closed, she moved her arm from over her eyes and let the tears fall. *Shit!* She never cried over a guy, and here she was, crying a second time over that damn Dedrick. He didn't want her, so why the hell couldn't she stop thinking about him?

Because you idiot, he got under your skin!

She rolled over to her side and faced the window. It was late. She should be sound asleep after the way she drank, but she felt as if she couldn't sleep. Jaclyn knew that if she closed her eyes, she was only going to remember again how it felt to be held in Dedrick's arms. Her body would tingle with the memories of the sex, and her senses would recall how good he smelled.

Jaclyn hugged herself as the tears kept coming and wished like hell it was his arms holding her in bed. "I've got to get out of here before he takes hold of my heart," she whispered to the moon that would be full in just a few days. "He gets that, then I'm a goner."

Her eyes became heavy, and soon she was falling asleep, but just as soon as it started, it was over when ice water touched her head and face and jolted her awake. Jaclyn winced at the sun that shined brightly in her face and shook off the water.

"What the hell?" she gasped.

"We're even. Now get up. We need to talk." Dedrick crumbled the paper cup in his hand and tossed it to the side.

"We don't have a damn thing to talk about," Jaclyn snapped, sitting up. "Damn it, Dedrick, you got my bed wet!"

"You told my brother."

She heard the anger in his voice, but this time she wasn't going to back down or apologize for her actions. "Get out, Dedrick. I'm not in the mood to have it out with you right now." She started getting out of the bed and shaking her arms that were still wet.

"Are you out of your mind?" he growled. "Why the hell would you tell him?" he finished at a yell.

moved her eyes up and down his body before stopping at his face. "You're right. I must be out of my mind. I fucked you, didn't I?" She turned and started for the bathroom, but Dedrick wasn't finished.

"Don't turn your goddamn back on me." He growled the words, letting each one rumble with a threat all its own.

She turned around and glared back at him, with her lips pressed thin with anger.

"First off, stop telling me what the hell I can and *cannot* do! And second, I was drunk. Half of what I said to Stefan last night I don't remember. So unless you have something important to discuss, there's the door. Please let it hit you in the ass on the way out!"

"You brought my brother into our mess, and now I have to straighten it all out," he grumbled.

"Oh, so now I'm a mess?" She placed her hands on her hips, facing him. "Everything that has happened couldn't have happened unless we both wanted it. So don't stand there and try to put all the blame on me, you piece of shit. In case your memory is a little shaky, let me remind you. I sucked your dick. You fucked me against the wall." She shrugged her shoulders, acting like she didn't care. "Over and done with. I'm moving on."

"You moved to a damn bottle like a coward," he snapped.

"Oh, go to hell, Dedrick," she yelled, picked up one of her shoes and threw it at him. "You have no right to judge me when you go running like a baby when a human gets interested in you." She tossed her hands in the air. "But guess what, you have your wish. I'm going to leave you alone, and as soon as Sidney comes back from her trip, I'll be out of your hair for good. That should make the big bad Dedrick all happy and cheerful." *I'm not going to cry*, she told herself as she took a deep breath. "In fact, I've forgotten about it already." She took another deep breath and forced those damn tears back. Facing him like this was starting to make her a blubbering fool. "Now, if you don't mind, I'm going to take a shower."

Jaclyn didn't wait for him to answer. She turned, went into the bathroom, locked the door, and leaned back against it. Once she let a calming breath out, the tears came again, and she didn't fight it. In fact, she slid to the floor as they dripped down her face.

She jumped when she heard the bedroom door slam shut, and covering her face with her hand, she cried. She didn't just let the tears fall down, but she cried hard until all that was left was the fight to catch her breath.

When the tears were finally over, Jaclyn took her shower. She turned cold then stepped out, wrapping a towel around her body. She glanced at herself in the mirror real quick. Her eyes were red, and she had this depressed expression that she had never seen before. Jaclyn never got this upset over a guy before, and couldn't for the life of her understand why Dedrick was turning her into a marshmallow.

Shaking her head, Jaclyn left the bathroom and gasped. Natasha was sitting on the side of the bed. "Natasha!" She looked around the room for her robe. "What're you doing here?"

"Here." Natasha held out her robe with a smile.

"Thanks." Jaclyn took the robe and went back into the bathroom. She dropped the towel and slipped the robe on, then went back out to see what Natasha might need. "Is something wrong?"

"I thought we might have a talk," she answered. "I don't think I've ever been able to sit down and talk to you without someone around."

"Oh." Jaclyn picked up her brush and sat down next to Natasha on the bed. She started to brush her hair, feeling very nervous. "So, what's on your mind?"

Natasha took a deep breath and let it out slowly. "Dedrick." Just one word was all she said, but it was enough to cause Jaclyn to stop brushing her hair. "I know there's some tension between the two of you and would like to know if it's something I can help you both with."

Jaclyn stood back up and went over to the vanity table. "I don't mean to be disrespectful here, Natasha." Jaclyn sighed, put her brush down, and hugged herself when she turned back to Natasha. "But I really don't want to have this talk with you."

"I understand more than you think." Natasha's voice was soothing and had the effect on Jaclyn that made her want to confess everything to her.

Jaclyn shook her head. "I'm sorry, but I can't talk about this."

"Then I won't force you, but I do feel like I need to say something, though." Natasha stood up. "Dedrick is not like Stefan or Adrian. He had to grow up fast. When his father died, he needed to be the protector of the family. He was a father figure to Stefan, where Adrian had one. I know you don't understand the no-human rule he has, and to tell you the truth, I don't either. What I do know is that he's very attracted to you."

Jaclyn snorted. "Could have fooled me."

"But he can't fool his mother!" Natasha smiled. "What I'm trying to say I suppose is that space is needed here. Not a lot." She wanted to make her point because Jaclyn was about to say something. "Just enough so he can think about what he wants for a change. Dedrick has everyone in this family needs and wants that I think he forgot about himself."

"I'm not his salvation, Natasha." Jaclyn hated how her voice broke when she spoke. She hated it even more when more tears threatened to fall. "I'm not the one to save your son, if that's why you came here."

Natasha moved close, but didn't hug her. She took hold of her arms and rubbed them in her sweet, motherly fashion. "I think you are very special, Jaclyn Davis. Don't ever let anyone tell you different."

* * * *

"Hey, where you two off to?" Stefan called from the top of the stairs to Jaclyn and Sidney.

"Shopping!" Jaclyn giggled. They had the boys with them as well, and she was playing with Brock.

"Shopping!" Stefan groaned. "I swear when you come for a visit my credit card gets maxed."

"Stop whining and I'll buy you something special." Sidney laughed.

Jaclyn laughed as well. "That shut him up."

"Can you get the pool ready?" Sidney asked. "We want to have a cookout and play with the boys in it."

"Oh, I suppose," Stefan answered. "If you bring it back in black."

"Stefan, you need a hobby," Jaclyn said. "Come on."

* * * *

Stefan shook his head as they left. He was about to go back into his room for a quick shower when Natasha caught his eyes. She waved him into her room. When she did that, something for sure was up.

"Ma?" he asked when he was close.

"Shhh," Natasha hissed, pushing him into her room and closing the door. "You and I are going to work together on something."

"Why do I get this strong feeling that you're about to meddle in something?" He crossed his arms over his chest and cocked his head to one side.

"We all have our secrets in this house, even you," she said. "I know you know more of what's going on between your brother and Jaclyn." She held her hand up when he opened his mouth. "I don't think I want to know either. But what I do want to do is help to give these two a little push."

"Ma, I don't think this is one of your best ideas." Stefan sighed.

"I think it is." Huffing, she stood as straight as her five-two frame would let her. "They just need a push. I think Jaclyn is perfect for Dedrick."

like the atom bomb going off again."

Natasha snorted. "His mate has landed in his lap, and we need to help open his eyes before it's too late."

Damn, what would she say if Stefan told her that they already slept together? Stefan would bet that his mother would either go crazy or start planning for another wedding. But if he kept his mouth shut, there would be a good chance that his knowing anything wouldn't ever come out. Stefan really didn't think that Dedrick and Jaclyn were a match.

"I don't see it." Stefan put his hands on his hips and shook his head. "She's not his mate, and I think if she were, Dedrick would see it and act."

"Horse shit."

Stefan spun and looked at his mother in shock. Not once in his life could he recall hearing his mother swear. Not even when she had been extremely pissed at them over things they had done while growing up. "Mother!"

"Oh." She waved her hand at him and started to pace. "We need something to get them together," she mumbled to herself.

"Ma, I think there's something you need to know." Stefan sighed.

"Something that makes them think and see that they're perfect together."

"Mother!" Stefan raised his voice and was able to get her to stop her pacing and talking to herself. "There's something you need to know."

"What?" She looked at him, and he saw the worry in her eyes. "Stefan, what's wrong?" she asked again when he said nothing.

Shit! How the hell was he supposed to tell her? He knew that when Natasha discovered that the tension between Dedrick and Jaclyn wasn't because they needed to come together, but because they already *did*. How was he going to tell his mother that the two of them had sex the night of the party? Damn, even he was still having a hard time coming to terms with it.

"Well…" Stefan shifted from foot to foot, his gaze roaming from the floor, the walls and finally to his mother. "Something did happen, and I don't think it's what you will expect."

* * * *

Natasha sat in one of the lounge chairs next to the pool watching as Stefan and Jaclyn played a game of pool basketball. On the other side of the pool in another chair, Dedrick sat with dark sunglasses on, but she knew who he had his eyes on. After Stefan told her that the two of them had slept together the night of the party, she now understood what about. And she was pissed off over it.

Mostly, she was upset that she hadn't seen it. Skyler and Adrian had had the same kind of tension the first time they slept together and he marked her. But Natasha knew for a fact that Dedrick hadn't marked Jaclyn. Yet, anyway. However, if what she was seeing now indicated anything, then it was only a matter of time before that line was crossed, and Jaclyn would be bound to him for life.

But then again, she was wondering about that since Dedrick seemed bent on staying as far away from her as he could get.

"You're deep in thought." Sidney sat down in the chair next to her, and Natasha smiled.

"I'm always deep in thought, dear." Natasha forced her eyes away from Dedrick and onto Sidney. "How are you feeling?"

"The medicine is working." Sidney sighed. "I'm starting to feel like my old self again. Guess I never expected to get post partum depression. How could I know I'd want nothing to do with Stefan? I feel so guilty now." Sidney turned and laughed at Jaclyn and Stefan who were now dunking each other. "I'm so glad Jacy has been here to help."

"Well, don't beat yourself up too much over Stefan," Natasha said, patting Sidney on the hand. "He understands that you are different and that depression comes for humans after birth. What matters now is that the two of you are close again."

Sidney nodded. They were silent for a few minutes, and Natasha's eyes went right back over to Dedrick. She knew that her son was watching Jaclyn. After what Stefan told her this morning, it made a lot of sense with the way he had been trying like hell to stay away from Jaclyn, and here was Natasha now trying to push them together. Maybe Stefan was right. Maybe the two of them weren't meant to be together.

"Can I ask you something?" Sidney broke into her thoughts.

"You can ask me anything." Natasha tried to smile again, but failed. She just couldn't stop the anger from surfacing when it came to what was going on behind her back. In her eyes, she saw the whole Stefan and Sidney mess as well as the domination of Adrian toward Skyler.

"Do you know what's going on around here?"

Natasha sat up in her chair when Jaclyn got out of the pool laughing. Right off, Dedrick stiffened in his chair, and his head followed her as she walked right past him. Yeah, he was watching her, and as far as Natasha was concerned, it was time she dealt with it.

"Sidney, I'm about to find out." Natasha stood up. "Excuse me."

Stefan and Jaclyn were headed and stopped them. "Family meeting, right now!" she snapped, then pointed her finger at Dedrick. "You, too. I want the three of you in the family room right now!"

She turned and stormed back into the house. This time, Natasha was very angry, and she wanted answers, and she wanted them now!

"Sit down," she snapped when the three of them were in the room. Dedrick and Stefan took the sofa and Jaclyn the chair. "Why is it that every time I turn my back on you two, the shit has to hit the fan?" Natasha paced in front of the large leather sofa that Stefan and Dedrick were sitting on side by side.

"I don't like where this is going, *little* brother." Dedrick spoke low and deadly.

"And you're not going to either," Natasha snapped. "You know you are the responsible one in the family, or at least I thought you were . . ."

"Why are we sitting on the sofa like we're ten?" Stefan whispered to Dedrick.

"Because you two have been acting like you're ten!" Natasha shouted. "I can't believe this." She sighed, sounding like a woman who had been drained of all her energy. "Dedrick, you *know* better."

"And just what am I supposed to know better?" he asked, frowning. Natasha answered him with her eyes narrowed. He turned in the seat toward Stefan. "You told her! You couldn't keep your damn mouth shut, could you!" he yelled. "And besides, I don't remember you lecturing when Stefan brought Sidney home." Dedrick charged right back at her but backed off when Natasha crossed her arms over her chest and shot him another pissed-off glare.

"This is about *you*, not Stefan." Her voice was low. "Do you have any idea what you've done?"

Dedrick looked over at Jaclyn who was frowning. "Happy? The whole fucking house is going to know now."

"Don't you blame this shit all on me, buddy boy," Jaclyn grumbled back. "I may have started it, but you finished it that night." She stood up, glaring at Dedrick, who also stood up. "Maybe you should have shown me this side of you to begin with. Then I would have known better when it came to fucking you!" she shouted. "I would have found someone else!"

"Oh, so I was okay to fuck when you had an itch?" he yelled back, his chest rising and falling with his anger.

Natasha took hold of Dedrick's arm and Stefan also stood up. "Dedrick, calm down." Things were starting to get out of hand. She the same room, she could resolve the mess, but it looked like all she was doing was bringing more problems to the surface.

"Yeah, that's right." Jaclyn tossed back, her eyes narrowing at him. "And now that itch has been scratched, so piss off."

"Enough!" Natasha yelled, silencing both of them.

Dedrick backed off. Natasha yelled only a few times, and when she did, there was no mistaking that her anger had reached a new high. She pushed Dedrick back down on the sofa and turned to Jaclyn.

"You sit down also." Natasha huffed. Jaclyn did, giving Dedrick a dirty look before crossing one leg over the other and her arms over her chest. "I'm not going to stand here and lecture. You all are too old for that, but whether this is a mistake or not, the fact of the matter is the two of you did sleep together, and we need to come to some kind of understanding here." Jaclyn took a loud breath in and an even louder one out, letting them all know she didn't like what was being said here.

"It was just sex," Jaclyn stated. "You three act like it was some damn commitment."

"It's not a commitment, Jaclyn." Natasha sighed, sitting down in a chair. "Shifter males don't do the one-night stand thing unless their heat is close by. Dedrick's heat wasn't close the night of the party."

"Well, my brother, you I do not envy." Stefan slapped Dedrick on the shoulder and smiled when Dedrick glanced at him.

"Oh don't get all smug on me, *brother*." Dedrick took hold of Stefan's wrist and pushed his hand off his shoulder. "Your wife is going to have your nuts in your throat as soon as she finds out that you knew about this and didn't tell her."

Stefan laughed, but it wasn't in humor. "You wouldn't?" One eyebrow on Dedrick's face went up with his answer. "That's blackmail!"

"Stop this, both of you!" Natasha once again raised her voice and stood back up to silence the two from arguing further. "Dedrick, I'm so disappointed in you. First, you forced Adrian to hurry up and mark your sister. You." She pointed at Stefan. "You're keeping secrets. Do you two idiots not see that meddling only makes things worse?"

"Wow!" Stefan placed his hands on his hips and snorted at his mother. "You were the one who…"

Natasha stopped him from saying more by rushing over to him and putting her hand over his mouth. "That's enough."

"Why do I have a feeling that this is something I need to hear?" Dedrick said cocking his head to the side.

"No, you don't," Natasha gasped. She gave Stefan a push, and he need to focus on the problem at hand."

Dedrick shrugged. "I don't see a problem. I'm staying away from her, and it's working."

"Yeah," Jaclyn huffed. "Maybe you should tell them you kissed me the other night then." She smirked.

Dedrick gritted his teeth together and looked up at the ceiling. "Not helping."

"Maybe I'm not here to help your sorry ass." Jaclyn stood back up. "Ever since that night, you've treated me like shit, and I'm sick of it. We had sex, people." She looked at them all, her blue eyes locking with Natasha. "It meant nothing." Natasha saw the pain and wanted desperately to reach out to Jaclyn but didn't move. "And it isn't going to go away or be forgotten if you three don't stop bringing it up."

"Jaclyn," Natasha said softly.

"Please, Natasha." Jaclyn's voice started to shake. "Just drop it. It's over." She turned and quickly left the room.

Dedrick stood up. "I'm going also. Don't set a place for me at the table."

Natasha didn't try to call him back. She slumped back down in the chair, her eyes on Stefan. "Did you see what I just saw?"

Stefan nodded his head. "But we can't push this, Ma." He sighed, rubbing the back of his neck. "They're both proud and strong-willed. It has to happen on its own or not at all."

"Even if they end up making a mistake by walking away from it?" She took a deep breath and sat forward in her chair. "Stefan, Jaclyn is hurting, and your brother is being stubborn."

Stefan stood up, walked over to her, and kissed Natasha on the cheek. "But we can't meddle this time. Let them figure it out. I'm going to bed."

Natasha stayed put in the dark. "Oh, Drake, I sure could use your help now with our boys." She sighed.

Chapter Five

Jason Spencer sat in a metal chair in front of the parole board waiting anxiously while they read their files to decide if he was going have to finish his sentence. Five years he'd spent in a small cement cell waiting for his chance to get out, and in those five years, no one came to see him. *That's okay*, Jason thought as he worked to keep his face masked of all emotions. *When I get out, she is going to pay for turning her back on me.*

At twenty-nine, Jason spent more time behind some kind of bars than he did out in the streets. He was sixteen when he committed his first crime, and because he had been a minor, he had gotten off with probation. Breaking and entering with assault was his crime, and his father had beaten the living hell out of him for getting caught, not for doing the crime.

Jason had kept it straight after that. Every once in a while, he could be found doing some bullying shit around the neighborhood, but nothing to bring him to the attention of the authorities. When he turned eighteen, his father married Lucy Davis. God, how Jason hated that bitch, but her daughter wasn't too bad to look at. Jaclyn Davis was thirteen when Jason came into her life, and from that day on, he wanted nothing more than to break her in, his way.

He was already six foot, the day he moved in, with shoulders like a football player and a mean streak from hell. It wasn't too long after his father was married that Jason noticed how the man watched Jaclyn all the time. Lucy also noticed, and it soon led to many fights in the house. Jason wasn't immune to his stepsister either. He'd had many nights that he thought about her, but at the time, the threat of his father's fists kept him in line.

It soon became known that Jason's father stayed married to Lucy in the hope that he could bed his stepdaughter, and that dream shattered when she up and moved out of the house the night of her seventeenth birthday. His father beat the hell out of Lucy for letting her go off to college behind his back. He then went out, got drunk, and wrapped his truck around a pole, killing himself. From that day on, Jason no longer had a fist to worry about to keep his temper and sick nature in line.

He was twenty-four the day he broke into a house and stumbled upon a young woman with her boyfriend who wasn't supposed to be there. She had decided to stay home and play sick so she could play with her boyfriend.

The boyfriend tried to call 911, but Jason ended up beating him with the phone, putting the poor bastard in a coma for about a month. He then turned on the woman, raping and beating her as well, then robbing the house. Three months later, he was picked up, charged, and it was off to jail for him. That had been five years ago, but it felt like a lifetime.

"Mr. Spencer," The director of the board called out, cutting into Jason's memories. He stood up, straightened his back, and willed himself to be calm and civil. "We have read over your file and must say that we were worried about you being released. The board didn't feel you were ready to go back out into society, but after this letter we received yesterday, we are inclined to give you another chance and place you under a guardian."

Guardian? Jason thought the question but didn't voice it. It didn't mean shit to him if he had someone looking over his shoulder all the time or not. He would ditch the guy later on, disappear, and never be heard of again. Hell, he might even change his name.

"So we're granting you parole." The man closed the file and stood up. "But let me make this very clear, Mr. Spencer. One more mess up, and you will be back here to serve the rest of your sentence without any other chances for parole."

Jason bit his tongue so he wouldn't tell the balding dick to kiss his ass. He nodded. "Thank you, sir."

* * * *

One hour after he was released, Jason Spencer stood in front of the thick gates leading to the outside world and waited for it to open. When the gate rose up, with each inch, Jason's grin got bigger and bigger.

He stepped out of the prison, closed his eyes, and took a deep breath of freedom. His peace was short-lived by the clearing of a throat that had Jason opening his eyes and snapping his head to the right where a long black limo was parked with a driver standing at the open back door.

"Mr. Spencer." The driver called out. "If you please?" He motioned with his hand to the inside of the car.

Jason walked to the limo, glanced around, then bent to see four legs, indicating two men were sitting inside waiting.

"Have a seat, Mr. Spencer," one voice from inside called out. "We have some business to discuss."

Jason moved to sit inside the limo and sat down on the opposite side from where the two men in fancy suits sat. The door closed, and his eyes moved back and forth between the two.

The oldest, a man appearing to be in his late sixties, had a cane resting between his legs with his hands clasped on top. He watched Jason, making him feel like he was sitting across from his father, waiting for a fist to land in his face at any moment.

He older gentleman seemed powerful, with a cruel side that he kept eyes, the need for payback and revenge. It was the same expression that Jason had each and every time his father beat the hell out of him.

Jason couldn't determine what his face looked like in the darkness of the limo, but the one sitting next to him, he could. The guy was younger, maybe in his thirties with the same kind of power coming off him as the old guy. Dark, cold eyes looked at Jason. Thin lips seemed to thin out more when he checked him out, but the guy had a sense of boredom about him too.

"I'm Conner Martin, Jason," the older guy said. "I'm the one responsible for getting you out of prison." Jason said nothing. He narrowed his eyes at the old man calling himself Martin. "This is my associate, Josh Stan."

"And what do you want with me?" Jason asked, crossing one leg over the other while he sat back in the leather seat, his arms stretched out on top.

"I have a business proposition for you," Martin declared. "One I think you will find quite agreeable."

"Is that so?" Jason questioned. "And why would I want to work for you?"

Martin leaned forward, the lower half of his face coming into view, and a cruel smile spread over his lips. "Because, Mr. Spencer, I have you by the balls. You can either work for me, and make a lot of money or you can go back to prison and be someone else's bitch, without your balls." He shrugged, sitting back in his seat. "Your choice, but I don't have all day for you to make up your mind."

Jason sat on the seat and thought about what Martin said. The old man had a point. He did want his freedom, didn't care what he had to do in order to keep his teeth and face intact, and he sure as hell needed a job.

He roamed his eyes over the two, taking in their clothes, the limo, even their watches on their wrists. These two had money, and if they were into some heavy shit to get it, why the hell not?

"What'd you want?" Jason finally asked.

Martin smiled and nodded to Josh next to him. Josh tossed a large brown folder into Jason's lap.

"What's this?" Jason asked.

"Your assignment," Martin told him. "I'm assuming I don't have to tell you who the girl in the photo is." He stopped talking while Jason pulled out a photo of a girl he hadn't seen in a very long time. "Your job right now is to find her."

"Can I ask why?" Jason couldn't tear his eyes from the large eight-by-ten photo in his hand.

"My daughter is close to her," Martin said. "And my daughter has something I want."

Jason smiled, his thumb rubbing across the smiling face of a girl he'd lost track of over the years. Jaclyn Davis. "With pleasure."

* * * *

Jaclyn couldn't sleep. No matter how long she was in bed with her eyes closed willing herself to fall asleep, her body refused to relax so she could. Instead, Jaclyn paced her room watching the dark sky, glancing up at the moon, thinking about the shit that was going down in the house, thanks to her. Now added to that was the message on her phone.

"Ms. Davis, this is Robert Gordon, your brother's lawyer. I just thought I would call and let you know that your brother made parole."

How in the hell did that son of a bitch get parole after what he'd done? In her eyes, the bastard should have been locked up for life, with the key thrown away. She shrugged it off, refusing to think about it right now. She had other problems at the moment, and his name was Dedrick.

Jaclyn didn't feel guilty over having sex with Dedrick. He was good, better in fact than some of her past lovers, and no matter what she thought of him she still wanted to go back for more. She wanted to have his arms wrapped around her, making her feel secure and safe. She needed him holding her but didn't have a clue how to get it. Hell, she had never wanted what she desired from Dedrick with any of the other men with whom she had hooked up.

That wasn't what was holding her back. Jaclyn was trying her damnedest to walk away because of her past. How could she tell these people who were so good to her and treated her as one of their own that her family and past were a big mess? That since she was seventeen, she had been running away from who she was as well as from a certain person. How could she look Dedrick in the face and tell him that while he had a mother who cared, she had one that hadn't given a shit if she lived or died? For as long as Jaclyn could remember, her mother had always thought of herself first.

Her mother had boyfriend after boyfriend coming through their door and in her mother's bed. When Jaclyn started to fill out, those boyfriends started to take notice of her, something that angered Lucy Davis. Jaclyn didn't know too much about her father then. She'd been told that he took off before she was born, and until Jaclyn was thirteen, she thought he didn't give a damn about her. She was wrong. The lie bite her in the ass. Jaclyn's father did care and helped her as much as he could. He was the one to send her off to college and give her the chance to make something out of herself. But Jaclyn still didn't have the chance to get to know her father very well.

While she was in school on her eighteenth birthday, she got a letter saying her father had been killed in a car accident. It was a shock to discover he had left her a huge inherence, making Jaclyn set for life. It was another thing her mother hated and tried like hell to take it away.

Jaclyn dressed, since she wasn't going to sleep anyhow and left her room. On impulse, she decided to go in and check on the boys and was not surprised that Sidney was already up feeding one.

"Hey," Jaclyn whispered, pushing the door open. "They still not sleeping through the night?"

Sidney sighed and shook her head. "Not with the early teething. I called the doctor but not too much to do about it." She smiled. "Another amazing phase. Why are you up so early?"

Jaclyn walked over to the crib, where Brock was lying with a pacifier in his mouth. He looked like he was chewing on it, trying to get some relief and go to sleep. "Can't sleep."

"There was a time when you used to tell me just about everything," Sidney said. "Now you keep it all locked up." Jaclyn turned, gave Sidney a quick smile, and sat down in the rocker across from her. "Talk to me," Sidney pleaded with her.

Jaclyn stared at the wall over Sidney's shoulder. "My mother died a couple months ago."

"Oh, Jacy!" Sidney exclaimed. "Why didn't you tell me?"

"You didn't need the extra stress." She tried to smile, to put on the front that she was tough, but it didn't work. Instead, tears came, and Jaclyn didn't understand it. All this time she never once cried for Lucy Davis. "God, look at me?" She took a deep breath and wiped away the tears. "All I seem to do lately is cry over spilled milk."

"Jacy, she was your mother," Sidney said.

"No." Jaclyn shook her head and stood up, one hand on her hip the other pressed to her forehead. She tried like hell to will the tears away, but they kept coming. "She never acted like my mother." Quickly she turned back to Sidney. "All my life she used me to get my father to support her. She never let me meet the man until I was thirteen, damn it! Oh god, Sidney!" she moaned, dropping to the floor.

Sidney got up, put Drake into the crib, and rushed over to her. She held her, and Jaclyn wrapped her arms around her only friend.

"Jaclyn, I've known you for a long time," Sidney stated. "And I with your mother or her dying. You cut strings with her years ago, so why don't you tell me what's really going on?"

Jaclyn pulled out of Sidney's embrace and stood up. She went over to the crib, looked down at the twins, and sniffed back the wave of fresh tears that threatened to come. She needed to tell her. Sidney deserved to know the truth, no matter what Dedrick or Stefan thought.

She nodded her head and took a deep breath, but she couldn't meet Sidney's eyes. Not yet. "Okay. I'll tell you," she said softly. "I had sex with Dedrick the night of the party."

"Uh…uh…excuse me, but did I just hear you say you had sex with Dedrick?" Sidney frowned.

"Yes." Jaclyn nodded, closing her eyes. She was afraid to look at Sidney, afraid of what she might see in her best friend's eyes.

"Oh boy," Sidney said in a broken whisper.

"Sid…"

"Well that sure does explain the way the two of you have been acting," Sidney went on, pressing her hand to her forehead. "Does Stefan know?"

Jaclyn finally turned and bit the inside of her mouth. "It came out the night he picked me up drunk from the bar." Sidney opened her mouth in a silent *O* and Jaclyn went on. "Sid, I swear I didn't mean to hurt you or anyone in this family. It just sort of happened…and…"

"Did he mark you?"

The question seemed to come out of nowhere. Jaclyn was taken aback and thought about what happened that night. She shook her head. "No." She frowned. "Mark. What do you mean by mark?"

"Did he bite your shoulder?"

Again Jaclyn shook her head. "No."

Sidney took another deep breath. "Okay then."

"Just like that?" Jaclyn couldn't believe what she was seeing. After all the 'stay aways' she got where Dedrick was involved, she wasn't expecting Sidney to just say okay after she confessed to sleeping with him.

"Jaclyn, you're a big girl." Sidney smiled. "I can't tell you who to sleep with or who not to. From the look of you, you didn't get hurt afterward, and that was all I was worried about."

Another tear slipped down her cheek. "And what would you say if I told you I wanted to do it again?"

Sidney lowered her head, took a few deep breaths, then looked up at her. "Don't. I think he is only going to break your heart, Jacy, and I don't want to see that happen." Jaclyn nodded. "Now I'm going to try before these two wake up again. You should do the same."

Jaclyn stood in front of the cribs, staring down at the boys after Sidney left. She reached out and touched their heads as they slept. *He's only going to break your heart.* "He already has, I think," she muttered.

* * * *

"You look like a natural sitting there with two babies sleeping on your chest." Stefan walked out to the patio where Dedrick was sitting with both boys early in the morning. Tiny hands fisted in his long hair, one tiny head on each shoulder.

Dedrick didn't admit it to anyone, but he wanted nothing more than to have kids. He envied his brother, feeling a lot of jealousy toward Stefan for getting everything he wanted first. The mate, the kids, the love, it all seemed to land in Stefan's lap, making Dedrick wonder if it would ever happen for him.

The boys were so small in Dedrick's arms that he needed one arm under them to keep them from falling. With his free hand, he rubbed their backs or touched their heads. So far, both boys had light, sandy blonde hair like Stefan.

"They were fussing, so I brought them out here," Dedrick said, peeking down at them. "Sidney just fed them about an hour or so ago, so I thought I would take them since I couldn't sleep." He smiled when Drake yawned and pulled on his hair. "You're very lucky, Stefan."

Stefan took a seat across from him. "You'll have kids one day."

A thoughtful smile curled his mouth. Dedrick touched Brock on the head and sighed. "I don't know, man." He glanced up at Stefan. "I don't see my future like you did. Right now I can't even think beyond what is going to happen tonight with the full moon."

Stefan sat back and linked his fingers together over his chest. "I'm sorry I told Mom."

Dedrick met his brother's stare and tried to smile, but failed. "Don't worry about it. I should have known that something like that would have gotten out."

"Can I ask you why?"

Dedrick looked down at the boys again. Why? That question had been going over and over in his mind since the moment he had pulled away from her in the pool house. He couldn't answer it himself, so he knew that he wasn't going to be able to answer it for Stefan.

Why did he have sex with Jaclyn? Shit, if he only knew. "That's a question I've been trying to answer myself for days now."

Stefan took a deep breath and let it out slowly. "Have you ever stopped to think that maybe there is something more happening you want to admit?"

Dedrick glanced up at Stefan again. "I'm not like you, Stefan. At night, when you were young, you would dream of having your mate by your side in bed. When I was young, I would worry about who Skyler might be mated to and if Mom was ever going to go out again and find someone new. I don't see myself mated to anyone."

"Dedrick, you had sex with her for a reason, and I don't think it was just because you haven't been with a woman in a long time," Stefan stated. "There's an attraction there. Trust me. You've never been the type to just go out and have sex with anyone before. One night stands are not your thing. Adrian's yes, but not you."

Dedrick thought about this, and Stefan was right. He never had a one-night stand before. Past girls he dated for a while before they had sex, but with Jaclyn, something was different. The passion that was there that night was something he never experienced in his life. It was something he desperately wanted to do again.

"Want to know something?" he asked, looking Stefan dead in the eye. Stefan nodded. "I want to do it all again."

Both of Stefan's eyebrows went up. "Damn. Don't you think that tells you something right there?"

"Yeah." Dedrick nodded. "It tells me that I need to stay as far away from her as I can get." He groaned, letting his head rest on the back of the chair. "Stefan, she's human. I could really hurt her bad if she was around during my heat."

"Dedrick, you don't know that."

"Yeah, I do." Dedrick sighed. "I feel so out of control when I'm around her. I want to dominate her. Take and force." He moved his head and met Stefan eye to eye. "I don't feel like I can control myself when she is in the same room with me. What do you think it would be like if she was close as I'm going through my heat? I could kill her."

"Well, if you feel like that, then maybe it is best you two stay away from each other," Stefan said. "But, Dedrick, if you do discover that she is the one for you, don't piss it away. You only get one chance at true happiness."

* * * *

Jason rubbed the knuckles on his right hand. They were sore after the beating he had given that no-good pimp and his bitch of a whore. He paid for a blowjob and the girl couldn't get him off, then had the nerve to *not* give him his money back. In Jason's eyes, he paid for a service that wasn't delivered, so money back was a must.

He smiled as he drove his new car down the fancy block, looking yet for forty-eight hours and had already committed assault. Damn if it didn't feel good to be out again.

Jason had also impressed his boss. Ten hours after he was given an assignment, he had a name to hand over and was now following up on an address for that name. Martin was very happy with him. Even his right hand, Josh something, was impressed.

Even though Jason had been locked up for five years, it didn't mean he didn't have connections. He had his old ones, and he'd made a few new ones in the hold. Hell, he even paid a few cops a visit to call in a favor or two. It was great when men with badges owed you for a change.

Stefan Draeger was the name of the guy who had Martin's daughter. Brainwashed is what Martin told Jason, but he wasn't buying it. It didn't take a genius to figure out that his daughter left because her father was too damn controlling. Jason saw it. Saw the way Martin had to be in complete control and had to have things done his way. Jason didn't give a shit what Martin wanted or how as long as he was paid well for it. That name alone got him the money for his new ride, and once Jason got him the goods he was after, he would be set for life.

"Where the fuck is this place!" he yelled, glaring at the paper with the address on it again, but finding jack shit. Already he had been driving around over an hour, and each house to him was starting to appear the same.

Seventeen-thirty-five Sterne Boulevard was the address he'd gotten, but so far Jason wasn't having any luck in finding the street. The directions on his GPS unit told him that the street was this way, but Jason was starting to think the thing was defective, and with each passing moment he became more pissed.

Jason stopped at a street sign and yelled his frustrations. He parked the car right there and lit a cigarette. He was about to call it a night and go find someone he could knock the shit out of when a sign caught his eye. A dead end sign.

Jason got out of the car, walked over to the dead end sign, and smiled. Sterne Boulevard. But what had him smiling and walking around wasn't the fact that he had found the place. It was the fact that the address he had been given took up the whole damn dead end. Seventeen thirty-five Sterne Boulevard was a mother-fucking block. Stefan Draeger's home was literally a whole block with a large-ass iron fence wrapped neatly around it, and even a security camera fixed at the gates. There was no way they were going to be able to get inside that fortress.

around, Jason went back to his car and pulled out the cell phone that Martin gave him. He dialed the number and waited.

"It's me," he said when he connected. "I've found the house, but there's no *way* we're going to be able to get inside. We're going to have to find another way to get what you want." Jason smiled, putting his smoke out on the ground. "But don't worry. I've got a plan."

Chapter Six

Jaclyn didn't see Dedrick all day long. Stefan came down after noon and took Sidney and the boys out, but Dedrick stayed put in his room. In fact, that's where he seemed to spend most of his time.

Natasha had left the day before for the safe house, and Adrian and Skyler were due to come home sometime tomorrow. So, alone in the house, Jaclyn wandered around looking at photos on the walls. She spotted one that resembled Dedrick, at a young age, smiling up at a man who was more than likely his father. The man held a younger Stefan and Dedrick stood beside them and held up a large fish. Many other pictures were on the walls of Dedrick at different ages, Stefan and Skyler also. They all seemed like the happy family she knew they were; the kind that Jaclyn used to read about in stories when she was younger.

Jaclyn left the wall of photos, went into the kitchen, and fixed a couple of large turkey and ham sandwiches. She grabbed two cokes and decided to go up and face Dedrick. They needed to talk before his heat thing started, and this time, she was going to tell him what was on her mind. If they couldn't come to some kind of understanding, then she was going to leave and not come back, no matter how much Sidney begged her.

She didn't bother with knocking on his door, and wished like hell she had after she opened it and walked in.

Dedrick was lying on his bed, nude, the sheet barely covering his groin and the palms of his hands pressing into his eyes as if he had a major migraine. His clothes were scattered on the floor giving the appearance that he had tossed each article away as he removed it. He moaned and moved around like he was in pain, and that very impressive cock of his was stiff as hell. Jaclyn saw right off how still his movements became and his nose flared when he took in many deep breaths.

"Jaclyn." He growled her name softly. She heard the longing in his voice, and it bothered her that he was suffering so much. "You shouldn't be here."

"You, um, you didn't come down for anything to eat, so I thought I'd…um…make you something." Jaclyn walked over to the nightstand and set the sandwiches down. "Dedrick, we need to talk."

"Damn it, Jaclyn," he snapped. "Get out!"

"Fine." She snapped right back. Jaclyn turned and started to walk toward the door, but stopped, turned, and headed right back for the bed. "No, I'm not going to leave until you listen to what I've got to say, you asshole." She was huffing now, her anger coming to a boiling point. Jaclyn came into the room to be nice and talk to him, to try and fix the tension that was between them, but it seemed that once again, Dedrick was trying to control everything.

"If you don't leave right now…argh!" he moaned.

"Don't sit there and try to tell me that your heat thing has started, 'cause I know better." She placed her hands on her hips. "Sidney told me that it hits at night. It's not even six yet."

Dedrick was huffing, and he quickly sat up and swung his legs over to the side of the bed, with the sheet barely covering his body. "Maybe for Stefan." His voice became thicker and deeper, and when he looked up at her, his eyes were a deep red. "But for me, it starts in the morning." He didn't lunge at her, but Dedrick was fast in grabbing hold of her left wrist and pulling her closer.

"Dedrick." Jaclyn swallowed and licked her lips. She was nervous, and she never was nervous over anything. "What are you doing?"

Those dark red eyes captured hers, heated eyes that clearly showed his beast, need, and probably his heat. He seemed like he was on the edge, hard but the way his thumb moved back and forth on her wrist had Jaclyn feeling tenderness.

"I'm giving into this," he answered her. "You should have run when I gave you the chance. Now I'm going to get the relief I need from you."

Jaclyn swallowed hard. Her nerves were screaming to fight him or to crawl up on his lap. Dedrick looked dangerous to her. His eyes glowed red, and the way he moved his hands to her waist, fisted the waistline of her jeans caused her mouth to go dry.

"Dedrick, think about this now," she whispered.

"I can't think," Dedrick said, his voice thick and rough. "Hurts too much."

Jaclyn wasn't expecting his strength or his moves. He ripped the jean material right from her body. She cried out and tried to back away from him, but Dedrick was quicker and stronger, and he brought her in close. Her jeans were in shreds on the floor, and her shirt soon followed.

He held onto her hips, pulled her closer, and grazed his lips over her stomach. The contact had Jaclyn sucking in air and moving her hands up to his shoulders. She couldn't get over how hot Dedrick's skin felt and how tense the muscles were.

Dedrick touched her with his tongue and licked from her belly button up to the valley between her breasts. Jaclyn arched her back and moaned while moving her own hands up to his thick hair and raising her left leg up to his waist. Willpower seemed to go out the door for her. All Jaclyn could think about was crawling onto Dedrick's lap as his mouth moved over her body teasing the underside of her breasts, not taking the aching nipples into his mouth.

Again, Dedrick surprised her with his strength by picking her up with his hands on her bare ass. Jaclyn sucked in her breath, gasping when his hot breath and his wet mouth closed over her clit and pulled it into his mouth. Suspended in the air with Dedrick's hands on her ass, holding her to face level, Jaclyn had no choice but to stay put and take what he had to give.

Right before her orgasm hit, Dedrick tossed her on the bed with enough force that she bounced. Jaclyn didn't get much of a chance to do a damn thing before Dedrick had her legs, holding them by the inside of her thighs, parted as far as they would go, his mouth back on her pussy. He licked and sucked her hard, drawing out the powerful orgasm she was on the brink of having.

"Shit, Dedrick." Jaclyn moaned, arching her body up and fisting her hand in his thick hair. "Oh…yes…yes!"

His tongue plunged inside, and she came unglued. Jaclyn cried out her pleasure and tried like hell to close her legs around his head, but Dedrick held her open. He fucked her with his tongue and drove Jaclyn to a point that she was starting to think she might die from the pleasure.

The only thing she could do was hold onto the bedding over her head. Her breathing increased to a pant, and sweat beaded all over her body, but Dedrick didn't stop. He wiggled that wicked tongue of his deeper inside her and rubbed his nose against her clit.

"Dedrick," Jaclyn panted. "Shit…you're killing me!"

Dedrick stopped without warning and stood up. Before her eyes, she watched as hair started to sprout all over his body. But his red eyes intrigued her. Sidney had told her about the redness when they were in heat, but now, she got a real good taste of seeing it all for herself. What was before her was the one thing that everyone had been warning her about, and it turned her on like nothing else ever had. This was the wolf making himself known. This was the side of Dedrick they all told her to run from.

Jaclyn squirmed rubbing her legs together and touching her breasts. She licked her lips, and she was eating him up with her eyes. Her mouth watered at the site of his thick cock straining straight ahead.

"Okay, wolf boy." She slowly parted her legs again. "You can eat Red Riding Hood, but can you fuck her with that big bad dick of yours?"

Dedrick chuckled and stroked the flesh between his legs. "Forget already?"

"Refresh my memory."

"This wolf is going to show you exactly why Red Riding Hood should have stayed the hell away from the wolf in the woods."

She snorted, bit her lip, and sat up on her knees. "I think you're the sheep in wolf's clothing, so you are going to have to do better than that if you want to impress me."

Jaclyn opened her mouth and sucked the head of his cock into her mouth. She moaned at the spicy taste of his skin, the hot cinnamon that seemed to get hotter. Dedrick also moaned and tossed his head back. His hips thrust forward, but Jaclyn took the head, not the shaft. She was going to tease him just as he'd teased her, bring him to the edge of the cliff but not let him go over it.

It was Dedrick who pulled away and shoved her back onto the bed. Jaclyn had a brief moment to push her long hair from her face before he took hold of her ankles and spread her wide. One strong stroke, and Dedrick had his cock embedded in her pussy.

Jaclyn moaned. Dedrick filled and stretched her so much she felt a burn of protest with her muscles. It wasn't the first time she had sex with Dedrick, but damn if he didn't feel like he was thicker, bigger. The only thing that Jaclyn could put together for this was his heat thing must have changed his body somehow, or he did it himself when he changed in front of her. Either way, Jaclyn loved it!

Each stroke from him was a new caress to her senses. Dedrick managed to touch spots inside her body that she never knew existed. Her moan turned into pants and pleading when he moved. She could have grabbed the sheets, but Jaclyn wanted that extra feeling of closeness so she held onto his wrists, and when she raised her eyes up to his face, Dedrick had changed again.

More hair had sprouted on his body, and his normal thick muscles that she was accustomed to seeing seemed to get thicker right before her eyes. More stretching occurred with his cock, which made her body feel she was a virgin again. Even his height seemed to increase. Dedrick was changing, until Jaclyn felt like the man was no longer taking her but the animal in him was fucking her.

Dedrick's face was twisted in a frown, his eyes closed, and his mouth opened. His teeth changed, becoming sharp points in his mouth.

him had Jaclyn panting with excitement. She couldn't remember a time when she had been so turned on. She was immensely attracted to Dedrick's beast.

"Damn it, Dedrick!" She screamed in frustration. "Let me come!"

His eyes opened and he looked down at her. Bright red eyes that were so heated sent chills down her spine. Dedrick didn't answer her, only growled and snarled, but what she had said seemed to get her point across. With brutal force, he slammed into her, rocking the bed with the power of his strokes.

Slapping sounds from their bodies bounced off the walls to mix with the grunts from Dedrick, and within minutes Jaclyn was crying out. Her climax hit without any kind of warning, and still, Dedrick moved within her, making his animal sounds.

When her orgasm was over, Dedrick stopped and pulled out of her body. He was breathing hard, and it almost seemed like he was glaring at her with those red eyes of his. "You do know that each male is different, don't you?" he asked. His voice was deep but low as if he had a warning in it that she couldn't understand. "Some can fuck all night, but only come once." He took hold of her wrists, yanking her to her feet. As she stood, he sat down on the bed. "Others will fuck until they do come, and then they are finished until the next month." Jaclyn couldn't slow her breathing down or the excitement in her body. She jumped when he grabbed her waist and forced her legs open with his own. "But I'm different." She sucked her breath in and held it when Dedrick picked her up. "I fuck and come all night long and only stop when exhaustion hits. And I can't stop once I've started." He lowered his voice. "You should have left when you had the chance."

Jaclyn screamed when he slammed her down on his cock, facing away from him this time. The force and the roughness of the action was enough to have her climaxing again, and once again Dedrick pounded into her hard, forcing her to move through the pleasure.

She felt like she was about to have another one, with the way he was bouncing her on his lap, but never got the chance of getting it. No warning for Dedrick's release at all. His arms wrapped tightly around her body, and he surprised her by not yelling but growling. Dedrick also sucked on her shoulder, but not biting her, and because of the size of his cock, Jaclyn could feel the contracting of his orgasm too.

"I want you to ride me." The words rumbled against her neck as he spoke. "Make me come hard. Fuck my heat out of me."

Jaclyn wasn't able to say yes or no. Dedrick had her straddling him fast and had his cock now out of her, poised at her entrance, just waiting for her to take it back into her body. She took every inch he had.

Jaclyn didn't mess with much teasing and foreplay. She saw the need and desperation in Dedrick's red eyes and gave him what he wanted. She held onto his legs, arching her back, and moved her hips. She rode him fast, almost brutally, pulling out every sound that she could from his lips as she slammed into him.

"Yes, yes, yes." Dedrick groaned with each slam of her body, his hips coming up to buck under her. "Fuck my heat out of me."

Jaclyn wasn't able to make this ride last any longer than the first one. Once again, an orgasm hit, and she cried out, slamming her body down and hugging Dedrick as best as she could while she shook with her pleasure. His arms came around her, but she could tell that he hadn't come.

"You're going to be the death of me." Jaclyn panted. "But it's going to be one hell of a death."

Dedrick chuckled. "You don't really think I'm finished yet, do you?" She was about to answer him when she was flipped and positioned on her hands and knees on the bed with him behind her. "'Cause I'm not."

His strength amazed Jaclyn. Power and control was what he had, and she felt it each time he shoved his cock back into her. And yes, she was starting to get sore from the many times he used her, but she wasn't about to complain. For Jaclyn, Dedrick was the best she'd ever had, and in her eyes, he could do whatever he wanted as long as he kept doing it to her. Just being able to experience the pleasure again was worth any kind of pain she might have afterward.

"Do you know what I love, Jacy?" Her name purred out of his mouth and sent chills down her spine, but Jaclyn couldn't answer. All of her attention was focused on staying up on her hands and knees and pushing back against that amazing cock. "I love a good ass, and baby, I'm dying to fuck yours."

Jaclyn hung her head, her body shaking at his words. "I...I I've never done that before and not sure I can," she breathed out.

"You can," Dedrick growled. "And I'm going to show you how."

Jaclyn didn't see, hear, or feel him move to get anything, but she did cry out once she felt cold oil pour down the crack of her butt and his fingers rubbing it in and around the small opening of her anal ring. She tried to stiffen up when one finger pressed its way into her ass; but with the powerful thrusts of his cock in her pussy, it was hard to stand still and not push back.

voice no longer held humor or gentleness. What she heard now each time he spoke was a man on the edge.

"I've never done this Dedrick," Jaclyn repeated, with another shake of her head. Another finger joined the one that was doing a slow in and out motion. "Dedrick..." damn she hated how desperate she sounded and the way his name sounded like a plea.

"A little late to be crying Uncle," he said. "And I did tell you to leave." He moved his fingers in her, stretching her. "This is the animal taking you, baby. The word *no* is not in my vocabulary tonight.

He poured more oil down her backside and he pushed inside. She cried out and tried to move away, but his arm quickly wrapped around her waist, held her still. She was helpless to stop anything from happening now, and the sob she was holding slipped out when his cock stopped and slid free of her pussy.

Three fingers left her ass only to be replaced with the thick, heated head of his cock. Jaclyn couldn't relax and stiffened when he began to push his way in.

Tears came to her eyes when the tight ring didn't give, and he growled behind her, stopping for a few seconds. When his fingers touched her clit and he began playing with it, the breath left her lungs. He pressed his cock in more. Jaclyn couldn't stop the scream from leaving her lips, or was it a moan that left? The sensations that she was feeling at the moment had her unable to think about what day it was or the time.

Dedrick held her close without any trouble at all. "Relax," he coerced her, his voice low, sexy. She shivered in delight at the sound of his voice. "If you don't, it's only going to hurt instead of feel good.

Steady and with more oil, he pushed his way into her ass with determination. While pain mixed with pleasure, Jaclyn burned and felt as if she was going to be torn any second; and only when she was about to scream that she couldn't take anymore, he stopped.

"I'm in," he moaned in her ear.

Jaclyn couldn't say or do anything. She held her breath and waited as he slowly pulled his cock out until only the head remained. She felt more oil poured on her ass, which seemed to ease some of the burn, but once he shoved his cock back in, the burn was right back.

"Relax some, and it won't hurt," he told her.

Jaclyn tried to do as he suggested, to relax her body, and to work on her breathing, not holding it in. It was hard, but after a few more times of him pulling out, more oil, and a strong shove she was able to do it.

relaxed under him. Dedrick was moving in and out of her ass with so much ease that with each thrust, he started to pick up the pace. The cheeks of her ass slapped back into his pelvis, and his grunts turned into moans.

"Fuck, I'm going to come." Dedrick's voice changed. He sounded raw, like he might have a sore throat, and his thrusts were so powerful that Jaclyn wasn't able to hold herself up. Her face was down in the bed, and he held her hips up. "Motherfucker, I'm going to come!"

A deep, animalistic roar sounded behind her. Jaclyn cried out from the feel of his cock swelling in her ass, stretching her more. She did scream when his teeth clamped down on her shoulder, biting her hard.

He came in her ass, so much and so quick that she felt it spill out of her. Dedrick also collapsed on top of her, pushing her body the rest of the way down on the bed with his teeth still locked on her shoulder.

Time seemed to stand still, and Jaclyn thought she was going to pass out when he finally let go of her shoulder. His cock slid free of her ass, and Dedrick rolled over onto his back. Jaclyn did the same thing. She was so tired and drained, not to mention sore, that she didn't think she could even get up to take a shower, let alone pull the sheet up to cover her body.

"Shit." She sighed. "I can't even think of what to call that."

She closed her eyes and rested one arm over her eyes, trying to calm her body down. Damn if she wasn't sore, but damn if it all hadn't felt great! She felt him leave the bed and heard water running, but she just couldn't open her eyes to see what he was doing. If she had to take a guess, Jaclyn would say he was cleaning himself up, and that was fine with her. She didn't think she could do anymore anyway.

"One more." He purred the words in her ear right before she felt his body covers hers.

Jaclyn opened her eyes and looked up at him. Dedrick's own eyes were not so dark red and the light coat of fur on his body slowly receded. She didn't move as he positioned himself again between her legs.

This was the first time that they had sex in the normal position. Having him lying on top of her and slowly sliding his cock in was something tender and almost gave her some hope that there might be a chance for them.

His eyes closed again. "I can feel it going away." Faster and faster he moved his hips, his cock and pelvis rubbing her clit. "Son of a bitch, its coming!"

Dedrick reared back and came again, taking Jaclyn with him. It had been having tonight, but a smaller, more tender one. This time, her legs and arms dropped to the bed, and Dedrick had one hell of a time getting off her. He mostly flopped to the side of her, so tired he could hardly move it seemed.

"It's over?" Jaclyn asked, taking a quick glance at his body and his cock.

Dedrick had his eyes closed, his breathing still coming fast, body sweaty, and that impressive cock of his slowly going down. He nodded. "It's over."

Jaclyn managed to roll over and bring the sheet up to cover them both. "Good. I can't do anymore."

'That makes two of us."

* * * *

She was lying on her stomach, the sheet covering only her ass, hands under the pillow that was supporting her head. She was facing away from Dedrick, but Jaclyn could tell that he was still awake. Probably, like her, he was thinking about what happened with his heat and the fact that they had sex once again.

"You're still awake, aren't you?" she asked.

"Yes," he answered with a sigh.

"What happens now?" Jaclyn tried like hell to keep her voice from breaking and her eyes from tearing. She didn't want the answer but had to ask the question.

"I don't know."

Jaclyn glanced at the clock on the nightstand. Almost five in the morning, and she wasn't asleep like she should be. Her body was sore and relaxed, and all she wanted to do was turn into his arms, but she didn't.

"Things haven't changed," she whispered.

"No, they haven't." He groaned. She felt the bed move and figured that he was sitting up. Jaclyn took a quick glance and saw Dedrick sitting on the side of the bed, his back to her. "You shouldn't have come in here tonight."

Jaclyn also sat up and grabbed his shirt that was on the floor. She didn't look at him as she pulled it over her head. If she did, then she was going to break down and cry again. "Don't have to tell me," she stated under her breath. She stood up and walked to the door, still not looking at him. "I'll give you your shirt back later."

* * * *

Shit! Dedrick thought. *I did it again.* He winced when the door slammed shut but couldn't move from his spot on the bed. He hung his himself for what he had just done.

With a sigh, he stood up and went to the bathroom for a shower. He tried to shake off the guilt he had over putting his mark on her, but he couldn't. Things were just happening. Everything was moving way too fast for him right now. He was still having a hard time coming to terms with the sex in the pool house, and now this.

After his shower, Dedrick dressed and went down to the office. The house was still quiet, for which he was glad. He didn't want to face Stefan or Sidney and try to explain what happened last night. Right now, they didn't need to know that he spent his heat with Jaclyn under him.

He closed himself in the office and poured himself a large glass of brandy, not giving a shit that it was six in the morning. Right now, he thought of himself as a chicken shit and needed a stiff drink desperately.

As he swallowed the burning liquid, his eyes caught a brown envelope on his desk. He sat his glass down and picked it up. It was the information that he requisitioned about Jaclyn.

Jaclyn Celine Davis was written on the outside. Dedrick had done many background checks on people before. Hell, when Stefan told him about Sidney, he checked on her and discovered what kind of danger the family was going to face once Stefan made her his.

He picked the envelope up, ripped it open, and pulled out the information he requested and sat down to read it all. There was everything from what schools she had attended, her grades, and where she had lived. Dedrick had Jaclyn's whole life before him, but it was Lucy Davis that had his attention.

Jaclyn's mother was, in Dedrick's eyes, a pathetic excuse for a human. She had been arrested at least a dozen times for either drugs or prostitution. Lucky for Jaclyn she was born when her mother was still clean. A teen mother who turned to drugs and whoring to get by. It was a wonder to Dedrick how Jaclyn turned out so well.

He kept reading and was surprised when the name Jonathan McGrath stood out as her birth father. Dedrick knew of the family and had to wonder what Brent's son was doing messing around with Lucy Davis. For the McGrath family, she would be considered white trash. Dedrick also wondered if they all knew she had a child by Jonathan.

Brent McGrath was a well-to-do real estate man. He had lost his wife to cancer and had raised his only son alone. The reason Dedrick knew about him was that the company had sold the ground to Drake Draeger, who later built the family home. Funny how the world seemed so small at times.

Reading some more, Dedrick discovered that Jonathan did know about his daughter. In fact, he paid for her college and all expenses. Then, in his will, he left a very nice sum of money to her, which answered the question of how Jaclyn was able to live on her own for so long.

The last thing Dedrick read was a record that belonged to Jason Spencer, a stepbrother with a nasty assault and battery problem. Sitting back in his chair, he finished reading the information. Dedrick had a gut feeling that her stepbrother was one of the reasons Jaclyn didn't hang around too long. The other issue she had, which was trust, he would put money on was because of her parents. But something about the name Jason Spencer seemed to bug him, and he had to know why.

Dedrick, running the information over in his mind, left his office and padded on bare feet to the garage. When he had a lot on his mind, he tended to go out there and work on something, whether it was changing the oil on the car or doing something to his bike.

Dedrick didn't know how long he worked on it, or how long he stayed out there, but all of his senses picked up on Jaclyn as she came out to the garage.

"You son of a bitch!" All the information he had on her went flying into his face. "If you wanted to know something so goddamn bad, you should have asked me, not go digging around like a fucking peeping tom!"

"Would you have told me?" he asked, one eyebrow going up.

He was kneeling behind the bike, working on the exhaust when she stormed in. Dedrick stopped everything he was doing as papers went flying and slowly ran his eyes up from her boots to her smooth bare legs. She wore a short, tight ratty jean skirt that hugged her hips, bare stomach and up his eyes went to a tank top that stretched across her breasts. Damn she looked good. And she didn't answer him.

"The McGraths are your family, and your mother got pregnant with you when she was a teen," he said, stuffing his hands in his pockets. "Impressive family."

Dedrick thought he saw tears in her eyes, but nothing spilled. Seconds went by that felt like hours before she nodded. "So what!" she said through her teeth. "They are nothing more than a name on a piece of paper." She huffed, shaking her head. "You know, Sidney told me that you would dig into my past, but I didn't think you would stoop so low." She turned to leave, and that pissed him off.

"I need to know!" he yelled stopping her from leaving just yet.

Dedrick crossed his arms over his chest and just looked at her with no emotion. "That night in the pool house started all of this, sweetheart. You took full advantage of my weakness that night." He spread his arms out wide. "Since then, I've been fighting like hell not to touch you, and it's been one major fucking battle. And guess what? Once again, I get backed into a damn corner and end up right back where it all started. Buried so goddamn deep inside you, I can feel your heartbeat. Not once, or twice but many times, thanks to last night."

"I'm not going to do this autopsy with you." She shook her head, turned and went for the door. His voice stopped her once again.

"You're running again."

"Well, what the hell would you like for me to do?" she snapped. "You don't know me, Dedrick." She glared. "You don't seem to want to know me, and what you do know is that I'm good in bed with you and like sex the same way. So don't stand there trying to *Sigmund Freud* my ass. Until you've lived in my shoes, golden boy, you have no room to judge anyone."

"Oh, I'm not judging you. I'm merely asking a question." He frowned.

"What would you like to know, Dedrick?" Sarcasm poured out as she spoke to him. "Would you like to know that Brent McGrath paid my mother fifty thousand dollars to run off and have an abortion? I'm the dirty little secret in the closet."

"Your father knew about you."

"Ha!" she yelled. "He didn't meet me until I was thirteen. Want to know what his excuse was? He didn't know my mother had me! Why the fuck wouldn't she? I was her cash box. Once my grandfather found out I was born, he paid my mother for years to keep her mouth shut, and she did as long as the checks kept coming in. *I'm* the one that put a stop to it all when I contacted Jonathan McGrath, and I paid for that by the trash she brought into the place that should have been my shelter."

"Jesus," he muttered.

"Want more? How about this? My mother married this man who had a son. I didn't know this, but she had been messing around with him for a while, spending my child support money on him, and when he married her, he thought he was getting money." She huffed, her anger showing. "When my father started putting that money in an account for me to live off of, her new husband started to beat her. To this day, I don't understand why she stayed with him. I saw him beat her so many times and begged my father to take me away, but he wouldn't."

Dedrick bit his lip to keep from saying something nasty. He knew what families like the McGraths were. Proud. And if Brent's only son had a child out of wedlock to a girl that was not approved, then they would naturally try to hide it. But for Jonathan to come out and support her was surprising. That alone told Dedrick that he cared, probably more than what he was expected to, yet the man didn't care enough to take his daughter away from the abuse she lived through.

"His son cornered me one night," she went on, hands on hips. Those words had him stiffening. "I don't know if it was luck or not, but his father saw and beat the hell out of him for it. Later, I heard them talking about me and him saying that when the time came for me to be popped, he would do it first, and then his son could play. That was the only time my father did step in." She pulled back and looked up at him. "I called, and he came, and I've tried to never look back."

"Shit." Dedrick hung his head. Now he felt like an ass for digging into something that was clearly painful for her. "Jaclyn, I'm . . ."

"Save it," she spat. "You want the happy-ever-after shit that your brother has. And you want it with a shifter female." He looked up at her and frowned. "So good luck with that. I hope you have a good life."

Before he could say another word she was running back into the house, but Dedrick's gut was screaming at him that this wasn't over yet. Something else was about to happen, and it was going to start one hell of a fight.

Chapter Seven

Jaclyn quickly packed her things, and before anyone was up and about, she planned on being as far away from this place as she could get. She slung her bag over her shoulder and left her room, glancing behind her. She knew Dedrick had come back into the house and was in his room. He stopped at her door, knocked, and called out her name, but she ignored it. This time, Jaclyn was all out of things to say to him. She just wanted out and away from him.

She had changed her clothes, dressing in jeans and a shirt that would hide the mark on her shoulder. After her small talk with Sidney about being marked, she had a pretty good idea that nothing good would come out of it and was desperately hoping that Dedrick had forgotten all about putting it there.

Jaclyn was thinking about leaving Sidney a note, but figured she would just call her later to say good-bye and explain why she couldn't stay in the house any longer. She was pretty sure that Sidney would understand, or at least she hoped like hell she would. Silently, she went down the stairs to the front door. Looking over her shoulder to make sure that she wasn't followed, Jaclyn almost collided with Natasha, who was coming in with Adrian and Skyler right behind her.

"Oh." Natasha was surprised, but her smile faltered when she saw Jaclyn's bag. "What's happened?"

Jaclyn only stared at Natasha with her mouth open and backed up as the three of them walked inside, Adrian closing the door and blocking her way out. She started to feel like the walls were closing in on her, and she couldn't breath. She shook her head no and backed up some more.

"I...I..." Jaclyn stuttered. "I need to get out," she finally whispered. The room started to spin. Jaclyn dropped her bag and pressed her hand to the side of her head.

"Adrian, catch her!" Natasha cried out.

* * * *

Jaclyn slowly came to. The room spun a little, and she had a headache, but what stilled her was when she saw Dedrick standing at the end of the bed leaning against the wall with his arms crossed over his chest.

"What are you doing in here, Dedrick?" She sighed, sitting up slowly.

"Did you know that Stefan was always the prankster in the family?

The one that could go out and find what he needed and never worry about the consequences?" he said. "Not me. I was always the one that had to be reasonable and look out for everything."

"And your point is..."

"When my father died, I fell into the role of head of the house. I had to grow up fast. I had no choice in the matter. My family came first. Playing around for me was supposed to be over."

"So?"

Dedrick took a deep breath and let it out slowly. He looked uncomfortable standing there telling her this story, and for the life of her, she couldn't understand why he was telling it either.

"I was about sixteen when I went out on my first date. My father was gone, and I was coping and trying to be the head of the family. She called and wanted to go out, but I had gotten in some trouble and was grounded. My mother and I were having a power struggle to determine who was the head of the house. She thought I was too young. I had told this girl I couldn't, but she said she had a surprise for me, so I snuck out."

"Is there a point to this story?" Jaclyn didn't understand why, all of a sudden, Dedrick was spilling his guts to her.

"So I took my mother's car and picked her up. We parked, and before I even knew what was going on, she was unzipping my jeans and going down on me."

"What?" She gasped.

Dedrick nodded. "First date was turning out to be my first sexual experience. But she wasn't finished with me yet. We started messing around more and ended up in the back seat. I didn't know it then, but her father had forbid her to ever see me, and this was her way of getting even with him. She was a shifter female, and as we were fooling around, I discovered real quick how rough I could be during sex."

He swallowed hard, and she could tell he was extremely uncomfortable with telling her this story. "Anyway, things heated up in the back seat, and in no time my jeans were down to my ankles, and I was having sex with her when out of nowhere this light flashes in the car. I'm not going to go into the details, 'cause I'm sure you can figure out what happened. But when the back door opened, I came on this cop's shoes and fell out of the car at the same time."

Jaclyn couldn't help it. She burst out laughing. Dedrick cracked a smile, but it didn't last.

"Yeah, I can laugh now, but when he took me home and told my mother, it wasn't so funny."

this?"

"I hurt her that night." He sighed. "I roughed her up pretty bad and didn't even know it. I'm telling you this because, I think, what's going on between us is just about the sex, and I refuse to hurt you." He rubbed his face, pushed off the wall, and stuffed his hands into his pockets. "And I don't know what you want besides sex. With that girl from my past, I knew what she wanted, Jaclyn. With every girl I've ever been with, I've known! But with you, I have no clue. So, what I'm doing right now is asking you, point blank, what it is you want from me?"

Jaclyn looked at him, took a deep breath, and stood up. She walked over and stood in front of him. *Should I really tell him what I feel? What I need? Can I open myself up to that, or will I only set myself up for my heart to be broken?*

"What I want? You want to know what I want?"

"Spell it out for me." He sighed. "What do you want?"

"I want your arms around me each and every night. I want you to see me and want me as if I was the last breath you'd ever take," she whispered. "I want you to crave me, just like I'm craving you at night until I'm crazy with need to just be touched."

"Jaclyn . . ."

"I want you to fucking need me!" she yelled. "I want you to fall in love with me, for Christ sakes, like I'm falling in love with you." She couldn't stop her voice from breaking into a soft sob, or the words from spilling out.

"I'm not falling in love with you," Dedrick said with no emotion in his voice. Jaclyn slowly raised her head and met him in the eye. "I don't love you."

Jaclyn took one step back, swung her hand as hard as she could, and slapped Dedrick on the side of the face. "Goddamn you, Dedrick," she shouted. She slapped him again, and again, until Dedrick grabbed her wrist.

"Stop it." He sighed. But when Jaclyn didn't answer and only fought more, Dedrick shook her. "Knock it off!"

Jaclyn still struggled, and her shirt slipped to the side. Dedrick gave her another shake before he stopped and frowned, looking at her shoulder. He moved his hands from her wrists up to her arms, turned her roughly and pulled her shirt down more.

"You're hurting me," Jaclyn said, trying to pull away from his grip, but Dedrick only yanked her back to him. "Let go!"

"When did you get this?" Dedrick asked the question so soft that

Jaclyn wasn't sure what he said. She stopped struggling, frowned at him, and tried once more to pull away. "Jaclyn, when the fuck did you get this mark?"

"I don't know what you're talking about," she huffed as she struggled to get out of his arms.

"The mark!"

Jaclyn had enough. She was hurt on the inside and now on the outside, thanks to his rough treatment. Since she couldn't get him to let her go willingly, then Jaclyn was going to do the next best thing. She shoved her knee as hard as she could into his groin. He released her.

"Screw you, Dedrick." Jaclyn backed away from him, turned and ran to the door, yanked it open, and left him there. She ran through the hall, blinded by her tears.

* * * *

Dedrick dropped to the floor, holding himself in pain as Jaclyn ran from the room. He reflected on what could have happened last night while he waited for the pain to stop so he could go after her.

"Jaclyn!" Dedrick bellowed as he struggled to get back up on his feet. He managed to get to the door and staggered against the doorframe. "Shit," he hissed. "Jaclyn!"

She was running down the stairs when Adrian and Natasha came out of the dining room and looked up at him staggering at the top of the stairs.

"Adrian, stop her!" Dedrick yelled.

Adrian rushed after Jaclyn just as she reached the front door. Dedrick grabbed hold of the banister and groaned. Shit, her knee got him good.

"Let me go!" Jaclyn, struggling against his hold, screamed at Adrian. "I'm getting the hell out of here for good!"

"You're not going anywhere!" Dedrick yelled at the top of his lungs.

"Everyone needs to calm…" Natasha didn't finish what she was saying. Dedrick took hold of the railing and swung over the top to jump down to the first floor. "Dedrick!

"What the hell is going on?" Stefan ran out of the nursery, followed by Sidney. Each of them had a crying baby in their arms as they looked down at the first floor.

Dedrick landed on his feet and said, "Watch her knee, Adrian. It's brutal."

He walked up behind Jaclyn, took her left arm, and yanked her close. He had to grab hold of her right wrist at the same time to stop the contact with his face again.

"Get your God damn hands off of me!" Jaclyn was struggling for all she was worth.

"We have to talk," he growled. "Now!"

"I have nothing left to say to you," she snapped back, continuing her fight to get free.

"Oh we have plenty to say." Dedrick's voice lowered.

"Dedrick—"

"Not now, Mother!" Dedrick barked back.

Somehow, Jaclyn twisted out of his grip and moved around Adrian so he was standing between them. "Get away from me, Dedrick," she huffed. "I'm done talking to you."

"Adrian, move," Dedrick growled.

"Adrian, stay right there." Natasha put her hand up to keep Adrian right where he was. "Dedrick, what in the world is going on?"

Dedrick met Jaclyn's furious expression. His mind was rushing to recall all that happened last night. When he remembered the moment his mouth closed on her shoulder and he bit her he bit his lower lip. *Fuck!* He'd marked Jaclyn.

"Look at her shoulder," he said through his teeth.

Natasha frowned at him and moved to Jaclyn who was still standing behind Adrian. When Natasha reached out to touch Jaclyn, Jaclyn moved away, and Dedrick moved toward her. He grabbed hold of her arms, holding her back to his chest with his arm wrapped around her waist. He wasn't gentle when he pushed her long hair over to her other shoulder and pulled her shirt down to show the mark. Natasha sucked in her breath and Adrian groaned.

"Look!" he growled.

"Motherfucker, let me go!" Jaclyn struggled.

"Stop the shit, or I'm going to beat your damn ass," Dedrick hissed in her ear.

"Oh, Dedrick," Natasha whispered, her hand going to her throat, her eyes filling up with tears.

Dedrick gave Jaclyn another hard shake before he turned her away from Natasha and Adrian and started to walk her back to the stairs, or more like dragged her. "Get your damn hands off of me!" she cried out one more time. "When I get my hands on you, I'm going to shove your nuts down your throat!"

"Not if I shove them down yours first," he said low enough for only her to hear.

"Argh!" Jaclyn groaned and dropped her weight to the floor, but so he picked her up and carried her the rest of the way up. "I wouldn't touch you again if you had the last dick on Earth!"

Dedrick didn't take her back to her room, but to his, and was stopped by Sidney who blocked his way from getting to his room.

"What the hell is going on here?"

"Stefan." The name rumbled from Dedrick with the right amount of force that had Stefan moving.

Stefan came up behind Sidney, took hold of her with a baby still in his arms, and backed her away from Dedrick. Jaclyn started the fight again when he pushed open his bedroom door took two steps inside and kicked it closed. Dedrick put her down on her feet and with a little bit of anger, pushed Jaclyn away from him, then he braced himself with his feet apart, hands on hips, and his eyes narrowed on her.

"You bastard!" Jaclyn swung around, facing Dedrick with her own glare. "You have no damn right to force me to stay here after the way you just treated me."

"Wrong." He took one threatening step toward her, which had Jaclyn taking one back. "I have every right now. He kept coming, and Jaclyn kept retreating until her back touched the wall. She jumped when he slapped his hands on the wall next to her head and swallowed hard. "I gave you many chances to stay away from me last night, but you didn't listen." Dedrick lowered his voice, but the roughness was still in the tone. "It all had to be *your* way." He sneered. "Now the choice is out of both of our hands, Jaclyn. You're mine now, whether I like it or not *or* even want it."

"You're out of your mind," she whispered.

Dedrick moved his left hand and roughly pulled the shirt off her shoulder. ""I've marked you. The rules now have changed."

* * * *

Jaclyn looked down at her shoulder. Dedrick had bitten her, just like Stefan had done to Sidney. A crescent moon was on her shoulder, the mark that all the shifter males place on their mates when they claim them.

She shook her head vigorously. "No. No, goddamn way!" Jaclyn slapped his hand away from her shoulder and hit Dedrick hard in the chest. It didn't faze him.

Dedrick bent closer to her, and Jaclyn ducked under his arms. She put as much space between them as she could. He sighed. "It's a little late to be running away from me now, don't you think?"

"I'm not staying here," she told him, hugging herself and backing away from him. "You can't expect me to stay after what you said to me."

Dedrick growled, pushed off the wall, and swung around to face her. "I told you the truth!" His voice rose when he spoke to her, his anger was rolling off him in waves. "I'm not in love with you or falling in love with you. You want that shit, then you should have stuck with your own kind and left me the fuck alone."

"Bullshit," she snapped back. Jaclyn was still hurt over him saying he didn't love her. The way he sounded, when he said it made her feel he couldn't ever love her. So if a man couldn't fall for her, then why should she even bother with staying? "I watch the way you treat everyone in this house. You love them. You just refuse to open up to me, you dumb son of a bitch. You don't want a mate. You want a fucking lap dog to kiss your ass whenever the mood hits."

A satanic smile spread across his lips, and his eyes narrowed. "What are you trying to do, Jaclyn? Piss me off even more than what I am now?"

Jaclyn was taken aback. "Piss you off!" She huffed at the question. "And what the hell should you be pissed off about? You got laid with no strings attached to that cold black heart of yours. Me! I tried to give you something special, share something with you that I've never shared with anyone else, and you crushed it like it was mold under your goddamn foot." She gave him the once-over, up and down, and sneered back at him as he had her earlier. "I should have known a man like you would think with your dick, nothing more."

Jaclyn was so pissed she didn't give a damn what she said or how it might hurt him. He had crushed her only hope that something might come out of this strange thing between them. Great sex didn't make a relationship, and no matter how much she tried, it never would. Dedrick was Dedrick. Hard-ass shifter, alpha male. Who protected his family and never thought of himself. Looking at him now, Jaclyn understood that he would never give her what she desired the most. A man to love her no matter what. Not even her father could give her the kind of love she hungered for, and it appeared neither could Dedrick.

Dedrick charged over to her with a growl. When his hands took hold of her arms and jerked her close, it dawned on her that maybe, just maybe, she might have pushed him too damn far.

"What are you going to do, Dedrick?" Jaclyn demanded. "Hurt me to prove that you're a man."

"Do you want to know what kind of man I am?" He said the words between his clenched teeth. "I'll show you."

He shoved her hard toward the bed, and Jaclyn landed face first.

him, and Dedrick was working at the snap on his jeans. The animalistic expression in his eyes and the controlled manner in which he unfastened his jeans took her by surprise, because his actions were turning her on. Jaclyn didn't know what it was, but she had a real thing when Dedrick got all animal-like on her. The gruffness of his beast pushed her buttons, revved her up, had her wired and ready for anything he wanted to dish out.

His jeans were open, the bare head of his cock showed, touching his belly the moment he pulled his shirt over his head. Jaclyn swallowed and fought her desire that was surfacing. His arms were thick, stomach a washboard of strength. She knew she should be scared, but she wasn't. No, Jaclyn was excited, but she still had to put on a front. She couldn't let her body overrule her broken heart. She wasn't going to take the crumbs that he tossed her. If she couldn't have it all, she didn't want any.

"Forget it," Jaclyn snapped. "You're not going to ever touch me again."

"Wanna bet?"

She made to move off the bed at the side, but Dedrick was too fast. His arm snaked around her waist, and once again, he held her on the bed, on her stomach. She screamed and kicked her legs and squirmed under his hold, but that damn strength of his gave him the edge.

Her jeans were practically ripped open, then yanked down her legs to rest around her knees. Dedrick forced her legs to spread as much as her jeans would allow. Then he ripped her panties from her body.

"You son of a bitch!" she yelled at him.

"'Bout time you figured that out." His voice hardened when he spoke.

Dedrick's fingers dug in her flesh like needles as he positioned her on the bed. Pressing down on her neck he forced her to stay bent over the edge, legs hanging off the bed. Then he shoved a bed pillow under her stomach, raising her ass in the air, and her hair pulled over to the side. She hissed in pain from the pull of her hair as he held her like that and ripped part of her shirt to expose her shoulder where he had placed his mark of ownership on her.

She got no warning at all. Dedrick shoved his full, solid length into her, which forced Jaclyn onto her toes from the power of his penetration. She thanked her body for the excitement she felt, enjoying how he went all dominate on her, because if she weren't wet, and excited, he could have done some real damage to her body.

Jaclyn fisted her hands into the bed covers and held on as he used enough force that the bed thumped up and down on the floor. She had to bite her lower lip to stop the moans that were threatening to spill out into the room. However, she couldn't stop the scream of ecstasy from erupting out of her mouth with the orgasm that slammed through her. It was so powerful that she saw stars in the back of her closed eyes, and still Dedrick fucked her. One, two, three, and four brutal thrusts, and his teeth were sinking into her shoulder, and his cock erupted deep inside her pussy.

It felt so good having him inside her, and at the same time, it broke her heart. This time when the tears came, she didn't stop them from falling.

"As my mate I can do that to you whenever I desire," he said in her ear, breathing labored. "Remember that."

He pushed away from her, walked into the bathroom, and slammed the door. Jaclyn was shaking as she stood up and fixed her clothes, her face wet from crying again. She knew that he was right, just like she knew that no matter what, she was going to have to leave here and never come back. To stay and let Dedrick have everything and give nothing, was unacceptable to her.

* * * *

Dedrick sat at the head of the table, a frown in place, and glanced at Jaclyn every so often. Everyone was at the table for dinner, but not much talking was going on or eating for that matter.

He was disgusted with himself over how he had reacted to her trying to leave him this afternoon. Pissed he had marked her to begin with and royally pissed he couldn't control himself when they were arguing. It wasn't about sex, what he'd done. No, what Dedrick had accomplished by forcing her to bend to his desires was to show Jaclyn his dominance toward his mate. He needed her to know that she was now his, and all her fighting wouldn't change it. However, seeing her now sitting at the table, staring at her food but not touching it filled him with so much guilt that he couldn't stomach his own food.

"So how long do I get to expect this at my table?" Natasha asked. Her lips thinned with her own anger after she asked the question.

Dedrick fixed his eyes on his mother and rested back in his chair. "Expect what, Mother?"

Whenever he used *mother* toward her, Natasha and everyone else in the family knew Dedrick's mood. Short, cold words with anyone was all it took for them to know that he was borderline to raising the roof with his anger.

He looked at everyone at the table. Dedrick was waiting for anyone they all were quiet. None of them stopped from giving him a disapproving glare though. The only one at the table who didn't meet his eyes was Jaclyn. But if looks could kill, Dedrick would soon be dead and in his grave.

"You all wanted me to mate." He moved his hands out to the side of him. "I'm mated. Now everyone is pissed about it. There is just no pleasing you all."

Jaclyn pushed away from the table, stood up, walked around Natasha at the other end of the table from Dedrick, and headed toward the door.

"Where're you going?"

She stopped and slowly turned around. "Any place that doesn't have you in it."

Dedrick rubbed his face as she left and sighed. This was *not* how he wanted things.

"Happy now?" Adrian wanted to know.

"Go to hell, Adrian," Dedrick snapped back.

Natasha stood up and slammed her hands on the table. "Dedrick Allen Draeger. How could you break her like this?"

"Break her?" Dedrick gasped. "How the hell did I break her? Did you forget that she tried to shove my nuts up to my gut?"

"Don't you take that tone of voice with me! That girl reached out to you, and you crushed her. It's all over her face."

"She was falling in love with you," Sidney said. "I've known Jaclyn a long time, and she's never fallen for a guy before, or had any feelings for a man even close to this."

"Oh, so now I get to have the whole family on my ass for something that I had no control over," he said. "I *told* her last night to go away, but she didn't listen. She stayed in my damn room while I was in heat!"

"And I told you that first night that something like this was going to happen," Adrian added.

"We are not ganging up on you." Natasha sighed, sitting back down in her chair. "But this can't go on any longer. You need to fix the tension and hostility between the two of you."

Dedrick pushed himself away from table. "What I'm going to do is go up to my room and try to get some sleep. I think I've had enough of 'let's shit on Dedrick night.'"

Dedrick went upstairs and stopped at Jaclyn's door. He grasped the knob and turned it, growling when he found it locked. He didn't know what to say to her, to make her reconsider how she felt about him. He to her for his actions earlier. He shouldn't have forced her. Shouldn't have let his anger get the best of him. Instead of knocking and talking to her, he turned and walked away from her room to his own. He stopped short when he saw a note sticking out from under his door.

You were right when you said we're not right for each other. You're a shifter, I'm human. I should have seen that difference the first time I laid eyes on you, but as much as I tried to stay away from you, I couldn't. You are my weakness, Dedrick, but I'm nothing to you, and tonight, I think I finally saw that. I'm sorry I told you that I was falling in love with you. I know now it was the wrong thing to do. I hope that you will get everything you want, as well as the right shifter woman. I wish you the best. Someday, you will find the love that I feel for you with another.

Have a good life, Dedrick. The woman you pick sure will be a lucky one.

Jaclyn

Dedrick crumbled the note in his fist turned and rushed back down the hall to her door and banged on it. "Jaclyn! Jaclyn, open the damn door." *Bang—bang—bang!* "Jaclyn, open this door!"

"What's wrong?" Sidney wanted to know when she ran up to him, worry in her eyes.

Dedrick shoved the letter into her hands, took a step back, and kicked the door in. The window was open. She'd climbed out and left. He rushed over to the window and ran his eyes over the grounds to see if he could spot her off in the distance.

"Her stuff is gone," Sidney said. "She left everything we bought her." Dedrick turned with a frown at Sidney who was holding the letter and reading it. "She's gone," she whispered.

"What's going on?" Stefan said with the rest of the family behind him.

"Jaclyn has left." Dedrick turned and pushed past them into the hallway.

"Where are you going?" Stefan called out.

"I'm going to search for her," Dedrick answered.

"Dedrick," Sidney called out, stopping him. He turned back to her, waiting for the lecture or ass chewing he knew he deserved. "You won't be able to find her," she said. "Jaclyn is real good at disappearing."

Dedrick looked at Sidney, then Skyler, Adrian, Stefan and Natasha. Feeling the pain, pain that he never knew was there or could be felt, swell in his chest he said nothing for a few minutes. The pain of loss. The only time he could recall feeling it before was when his father died. It crushed him that night, and now he felt as if he were being crushed again. Maybe he was wrong. Maybe he could love someone and feel something for a person that wasn't a member of the family. Maybe he could love Jaclyn.

"Yeah, well I'm even better at finding people than she could ever be at hiding." He continued down the stairs. "And I'm going to find my mate."

Chapter Eight
Two weeks later...

"Twins." Jason tossed the folder on Martin's desk with a sneer on his lips.

Conner Martin opened the folder and stared at the photo of his daughter outside on a blanket in the grass with two identical boys sitting next to her with that thing she called a husband. Both boys appeared to be the same person, but Conner knew different. Just looking at the brats, he knew that he needed to get his hands on them and study them. If the children grew this fast, then there had to be something in their DNA, something he could use for his next experiment.

"It's going to be hard to get your hands on one of them too," Jason went on. "Her husband goes with her just about everywhere, and the gates are always locked. No fucking way to get in."

"There is always a way, Mr. Spencer." Martin sighed. "And I don't want one. I want them both." He closed the folder and looked up at the man he'd hired.

Jason Spencer. The man was the worst excuse for a human being, but the kind that Martin needed to get this job done. Jason didn't give a shit about who he hurt or killed to make a buck and Martin was paying the bastard a great deal of money. Over the years, he'd learned about the low percentage of humans being able to breed with one of those animals. So for Sidney to conceive not one but twins was something very impressive. Those two were special, and Martin wanted them in his lab ASAP.

"What I know about my daughter, Mr. Spencer, is that she doesn't play by the rules. No matter who sets them before her." Martin opened the folder once again and stared at Sidney's smiling face. "She'll have her guard down very soon, and when she does you will be there to remind her that following the rules is always the best thing." Martin glanced back up at Jason. "So when their guard is down, you will bring me what I desire. Understood?"

Jason smiled. "No problem."

Martin gave him a satisfied glare. "Good. You can go."

Josh Stan, who had been standing off to the side while Jason reported, strolled up to one of the leather chairs in front of the desk and sat down. Martin waited a few minutes, studying the photo before he acknowledged him.

"You have something on your mind?" Martin asked, sitting back in his chair and linking his fingers together over his stomach.

"Spencer is a loose cannon," Josh stated. "I don't trust him."

Martin nodded his head. "Good. I don't want you to."

"Then why is he here?" Martin heard the impatience in Josh's voice.

"Because he's perfect for this kind of job." Martin sat forward, opened a drawer, and pulled a file out. He tossed it to Josh. "He was Jaclyn's stepbrother, a long time ago. I checked into his background. Lust for something you can't have is a powerful motivator." He chuckled. "You can cage your pets, Josh, but to train them...now that takes skill." Martin stood and walked over to his wet bar. He poured two glasses of bourbon and handed one to Josh. "Train your pet right, Josh, and he'll be as loyal as a tamed kitten."

Josh took a drink, his eyes following Martin back to his chair. "So what is your plan for the girl?"

Martin set his drink on the desk. Linking his fingers together, he rested his chin on his hands and took a deep breath. "For now, we keep her drugged. I suspect that she has messed around with one of those things, and soon we will do the tests to prove it." He answered after some time went by. "What I want is them." He put his finger on the photo of the twins. "They are going to help bring forth my next project." He tossed a file at Josh. "And you're in charge of it."

Josh read the file and his eyes got huge. "Are you serious?"

Martin nodded. "It's time things changed, and in order to do that I need to know everything about them. You are to go to the lab and get it all set up. I'll bring you the sample as soon as I get it."

* * * *

"They are officially walking and talking." Sidney walked into the dining room with one boy on each hip. She handed one to Stefan. "I just snuck in their room, and they were walking around and mumbling. The moment they saw me, they dropped to the floor and started the baby jibberish."

"No shit?" Stefan said in surprise. "Well, the doc did say they would be doing that soon."

"Yeah, and Drake has a cold," Sidney told them. "So you're going to have to take us to the doctor."

"Oh... Sid..." Stefan stuttered and looked at Dedrick, who was sitting at the head of the table with a beer in his hand and about five empty bottles on the table. "I...um, sort of promised to help Dedrick check out a couple places that Jaclyn might be at."

said. "I can go alone."

Sidney glared at Dedrick. "How long are you going to sit around drinking and hoping that she's going to come back?"

"Maybe I'm drinking because I know she isn't," Dedrick replied in despair.

"I can go with you." Skyler chuckled. "Need to get out of the house anyway."

"It's your own damn fault," Sidney snapped, ignoring Skyler. "If you hadn't been such a stubborn ass, then she wouldn't have left."

"Sidney, don't," Stefan warned.

"So you're going to blame this shit on me?" Dedrick charged, sitting up in the chair. "I didn't tell your damn friend to come into the pool house, watch me strip, then suck my dick."

"No," Sidney yelled back. "You're just the one that fucked her against the wall." Sidney handed the baby to Skyler and put her hands on her hips. "Just admit it, Dedrick. You care for her and screwed it all up with your damn pride."

Sidney turned her back on them and started to walk out of the room, but Dedrick stood up and threw his bottle of beer hard against the wall. It shattered, and beer went all over.

"Don't judge me." Dedrick spoke low and sounded dangerous. "Don't you stand there and fucking *judge* me when your father is trying to kill each and every one of us. I have given everything I have to protect my family and you!"

"What happened?" Natasha rushed into the dining room, Adrian right behind her.

Dedrick turned his back on Sidney and left. She let out the breath she didn't even realize she was holding.

"Dedrick blew his top." Stefan sighed, glancing at Sidney.

"Oh, no, you don't." Sidney shook her head. "You are not going to blame that one on me. Everyone has been thinking it, and I just said it. You should have told me he was so sensitive right now."

"I told you don't," Stefan snapped.

"So what, we're supposed to treat him with kid gloves now?" Sidney yelled. "He broke her damn heart, and now I don't know where my best friend is."

"And she crushed him by walking out!" Stefan yelled back.

"Stefan, please." Natasha butted in. "She doesn't understand."

"Understand what?" Sidney huffed. "That Dedrick is a prick? Sure I do."

"It's not just that." Natasha sighed, glancing at Adrian.

"Sid, do you remember when Skyler sort of rejected me?" Adrian said.

"Sort of." Skyler huffed. "I did!"

Adrian rolled his eyes and shot her a glare. "You know what I mean," he said to her before turning back to Sidney. "When I left, I was broken. My mate had rejected me after I marked her, and I ended up hurting her just as much when I walked out."

"What's that got to do with anything?" Sidney sighed.

"It's the same thing between Jaclyn and Dedrick," Stefan said. "He may be having a hell of a time coming to terms with the marking and his feelings for her, but when she walked away, it's like he took another punch in his gut."

"Shifter males are very prideful," Natasha added. "Dedrick is the alpha of our pack, if that makes it more understandable. He may not have wanted to mark Jaclyn or claim her as his mate, but nature did it for him."

"In other words, Sid"—Skyler smiled—"Dedrick was starting to come to terms with his feelings for Jaclyn, and she bolted before he realized it."

"So I embarrassed him then?" Sidney frowned.

Skyler nodded. "In a way, yes."

Sidney took Drake back in her arms and shook her head. She couldn't believe that after the way Dedrick treated Jaclyn they were all taking his side and babying him. If he was in pain over Jaclyn leaving, then good! He should be hurting, because if Sidney knew Jaclyn as well as she thought she did, then she knew Jaclyn was probably passed out somewhere trying to drink him away.

"You know, do what you want. I have to take Drake to the doctor, and I'm going alone." She turned and headed for the door.

"Sid!" Stefan called out, but she ignored him.

* * * *

Jason sat in his car watching the property, waiting for the one chance he needed to grab the brats that Martin wanted. The kids meant nothing to him, but Jaclyn on the other hand, now that was the prize he wanted. Jason had some unfinished business with his stepsister. Business that needed to be dealt with soon.

"Well, what do you know?" Excitement hit him when he pulled the binoculars up to his eyes to look at the house and saw Martin's kid loading up one of the twins, alone. "Come to daddy." Keeping his eyes on them, he dug his phone out and dialed the boss. One was better than none in his eyes, and he sort of figured that this was going to be his brats. "It's me. I think I have an opening. Have the van ready, and I'll call you back. You're about to get a treat."

Jason hung up. He started the car and waited. Unbelievable excitement raced through him. He was getting some action that went right to his cock. He was hard, but this time Jason wasn't going to waste it on some whore. No, he was going to save this for someone very special. What had him frowning though was that Jaclyn wasn't with Sidney Martin.

He followed the Mercedes with a glare. This bitch had everything and Jason had to work just to get what he had. It wasn't fair, and the more he drove, following them, the angrier he got. Even Martin had it all, giving Jason scraps.

Jason rubbed his cock through his jeans as he thought of his sweet stepsister and wondered where in the hell she might be. He remembered the way she used to walk around the apartment in her tight shorts and even tighter shirts. Designer clothes that only she could afford to wear. Her daddy had money. The rest of the household had squat. Lucy didn't even get any of the damn money after she married his father.

When Jaclyn's daddy found out about Andy and Jason moving in, the money tree was chopped down. That was the reason the beatings started in the house. Andy Spencer wanted the money Lucy Davis's daughter was getting. He was pissed he couldn't get his hands on it, or Jaclyn either. With each passing year, Jason watched his father's lust increase along with his greed.

But Andy Spencer wasn't around anymore. Jason had free rein to go after the one bitch who had slipped through his fingers. Jaclyn. And once he had his hands on her, he was going to make her pay for all the years he not only spent in jail, but also for the time away from her. If Jason could love, then Jaclyn would be his love, but he knew he couldn't. He loved no one and nothing but money and pain. And the more he had of both, the better. But right now, he was seeing red. Jaclyn was supposed to be in that car with Sidney, but she wasn't.

He followed the car to a doctor's office. Jason parked on a side road about a half block down got out and leaned back on the hood of his car watching. Sidney took the one kid out of the back seat, kissed his head, and walked into the office.

Jason pulled his phone out and hit redial. "Doctor's office. Ninety-sixty Fifth Street. South side. Make it fast if you want the prize." He hung up and, in a casual manner, walked across the street to wait.

Twenty minutes went by before a dark van pulled up. Jason

driver to head over to the Mercedes. They waited for almost an hour before Sidney came back out with the kid.

Jason waited until they were close to the car before he came out of his hiding spot, the adrenaline rushing and his cock stiff and knuckles aching to hit something. He walked right up to Sidney from behind, waiting for a second for her to turn to face him before he snatched the boy out of her hands, and tossed him to one of the waiting guys.

"I'll take that," he said, when she turned around.

Sidney opened her mouth to scream when Jason backhanded her so hard she went down to the ground. The kid started screaming.

Everything happened so fast. The boy was practically thrown into a small cage in the van, tires squealed as it peeled out of the parking lot. Jason knelt down, hovering over Sidney who was still in a daze over the slap he gave her.

"Where's Jaclyn?" Jason asked. When she didn't answer, he grabbed a fist full of her hair and jerked her around. "I asked you a question, bitch."

"Someone help me!" Sidney screamed. "He kidnapped my baby!"

Jason snarled and hit her again with his closed fist, which shut her up. "I'm going to find her," he said, his face mere inches from hers. Jason had smacked Sidney so hard she started to close her eyes. "And when I do I'm going to fuck her up, just like she fucked me over. And your daddy says thank you for the specimen." He chuckled right before her eyes closed. He brought out the phone again while he jogged to the car. "I've got one," he said into the phone.

* * * *

"She has a concussion, a bruise on her left cheek, and a busted lip," Stefan told Dedrick, his eyes red with anger when he looked at him. "She also had to be sedated, and Skyler is trying to get Brock to calm down."

Dedrick stopped pacing his office, finished his drink in one gulp, and frowned at his brother. A local policeman had called the house to tell them that Sidney was in the hospital, hysterical and mumbling something about Drake being gone. There was no doubt in their minds, when Dedrick and Stefan heard what the officer had to say, they both knew that Drake had been kidnapped. Conner Martin had taken his grandchild. At the hospital, before Sidney fell asleep, she told them the man responsible for taking Drake was looking for Jaclyn too. Dedrick would put his last dollar on the line that the man hunting Jaclyn's whereabouts was Jason Spencer.

"Mom with her?" Dedrick tried to keep his voice level and failed.

Rage filled him.

"Yeah," Stefan answered. His own voice shook with anger to go with the red in his eyes. "She's keeping ice on Sid's face for the swelling." Stefan ran his hands in his hair and growled. "He hit her and stole my child. I want to kill that fucker so bad!" he snarled.

"I'm sorry about what I said to Sidney this morning," Dedrick said, the guilt eating him alive. "I didn't mean it."

"I know you didn't." Stefan tried to smile, but failed. "It's been so crazy around here for so long."

"I should have seen what was in front of me," Dedrick went on. "But I was so worried about hurting another human."

"Okay, boys, let me show you how I play with my toys." Adrian walked into the office with a laptop computer in his hands, another small black box, and a bunch of wires. "Some assistance would be appreciated."

Dedrick rolled his eyes and went over to help Adrian set the computer up on his desk. "I hope you have a plan."

"Have I ever let you down?" Adrian smirked. "I told you that I would help you locate Jaclyn with the help of her cell phone. Now as soon as Sidney wakes up have her call her nutty dad and I can lock in on him as well."

"Who would have ever thought he could do a hack." Stefan thumbed at Adrian.

"Sweetheart, I'm full of surprises." Adrian smiled. "Now watch and learn boys."

"Stefan, I can't get him to calm down." Skyler walked into the office with Brock, who was screaming at the top of his lungs. His face was red, and he was squirming in Skyler's arms.

"Come here, buddy," Stefan said to him, taking the boy, and walking him to the other side of the office.

Dedrick watched his brother comfort the baby. He heard him say things like "Momma was only taking a nap," and "Drake would be home soon." It seemed to help some. Brock did calm down enough that he rested his head on Stefan's shoulder, but the tears and sniffling were still there.

The boys shared a link not only with each other, but with their mother as well. Until they reached one year old, they would always know what was going on as if they were still in her womb. So for Sidney to be upset over Drake getting kidnapped, Brock and Drake both were going to be upset as well, but with Drake also gone, Brock was practically in a panic state.

arrested for that, I'm not bailing you out," Skyler said to Adrian, leaning over his shoulder.

"Only if I get caught, baby," Adrian charmed back.

"I'll bail your ass out," Dedrick said. When Skyler glared at him, he winked at her.

"My hero." Adrian sighed, his fingers not missing a key as he typed.

"I think Jason Spencer is working for Martin," Dedrick said after a few minutes of silence went by.

"Jason who?" Stefan asked.

Dedrick turned to Stefan. The guilt was bothering him bad. Watching Stefan rub Brock's back and sway back and forth to keep him calm was killing Dedrick. He felt like all of this was his fault. Sidney left alone, mad, and now Drake was gone, just like Jaclyn.

"Jason Spencer." Dedrick sighed. "He's Jaclyn's stepbrother. Just got out of jail a few weeks ago, on parole. I dug around, and he has a benefactor who picked him up the day he was released. I bet anything it was Martin."

"Why the hell would Martin want him?" Stefan asked with a frown.

"Because Jason wants Jaclyn, and Jaclyn is close to Sidney," Skyler added. Both Stefan and Dedrick turned to Skyler. "What?"

"How would you know?" Dedrick asked.

"Because Jaclyn talked to me one night." Skyler shrugged. She rolled her eyes, as though she was very uncomfortable. "I shouldn't be telling you this, because it's only going to put you into a rage."

"Tell me, Sky," Dedrick said, his gut dropping.

"Jason tried to rape her," Skyler said, glancing over to Dedrick to see how he was taking this bit of news. "After the night Jason's father tried to molest her, Jaclyn's father took her away. Jason broke into the hotel where he'd taken her and tried to rape her. It was her father coming back to check up on her that saved her from being raped."

"That motherfucker!" Stefan said through his teeth.

"I already knew." Dedrick sighed.

"Oh this just gets better." Stefan chuckled, but it wasn't in humor.

"Got you!" Adrian yelled, slapping his hands together. "Her cell phone is giving off a signal." He looked up at Dedrick. "Old hospital about forty-five minutes from here."

"I'm going," Dedrick said and turned to leave. He was going to bring his mate home if he had to carry her kicking and screaming all the way, he thought. Jaclyn was going to come home and he was going to do everything he could to make this shit up to her. "Text me the address."

"Dedrick!" Adrian yelled, stopping him. "You should look at this."

Dedrick turned and headed back to Adrian, hovering near his shoulder. Adrian pointed to the owner of the property. Conner Martin.

"Son of a bitch!" Skyler said.

Dedrick didn't say a thing. He looked at the name on the deed, the address, and the flashing light, which told him that it was Jaclyn's cell phone. If her phone was there, in his building, then she wasn't there willingly. The question that kept running through his mind—had Jaclyn been there all this time? And if so, what was that bastard doing to her?

"I'm going to kill him," Dedrick said turning to walk out of the room.

Adrian flew out of the chair, rushed him, and stood right in front of Dedrick blocking him from leaving the room. "You're not going anywhere with that look in your eye, man."

"Get out of my way, Adrian," Dedrick ordered in a low, deadly voice.

"I can't let you go out there right now," Adrian said. "You're not right in the head at the moment."

Dedrick moved, and Adrian tackled him to the floor. Brock started screaming again, and just when Dedrick almost had Adrian off him, Stefan came to help. Together, they pinned him down and sat on him.

Dedrick yelled at the top of his lungs.

"Skyler, get Brock out of here." Stefan huffed as he struggled with Dedrick. "He's only getting upset again."

Skyler hurried from the room with Brock screaming again while Adrian and Stefan fought to hold Dedrick down. Dedrick couldn't stop the raging screams from coming. His mate was in danger. He knew it, could feel it, and he wanted blood to spill for it. He wanted to put his hands around that bastard's throat and rip it out.

He didn't know how long he fought with them, but only when Dedrick finally let his rage go and cried did the two men release him.

Stefan hugged him, then and Dedrick cried. It was the first time he shed tears since the death of his father. That was the last night he ever cried, and it was in the arms of his mother. Now he shed them on his brother's shoulder, and he didn't give a damn that Adrian was there.

How could he have been so stupid? Dedrick knew Jaclyn was his. He had figured it out when she came for a visit after Skyler and Adrian mated, but he was too damn stubborn to accept it. Just because she was human. He pushed her away so many times, and now when he needed her, she wasn't here. She was out there, maybe hurt, and it was all because of him.

"I can't lose her now," Dedrick whispered against Stefan's shoulder. "I'll die.

"You're not going to lose her," Stefan assured him. "You're going to get your shit together, and we're going to bring our family back home."

Dedrick nodded.

"Now, if we're done with the drama." Adrian knelt down and handed Dedrick a glass of brandy. "I say have a drink, and let's find out where good old Martin is. Because I don't know about you two, but I'm now itching to blow something up." He finished with a smile.

* * * *

Jason walked down the damp basement that led to some medical set up Martin had put together for some shit that Jason didn't give a fuck about. Behind him were the men that came to help him with the kidnapping, one holding a crying kid.

"Get your fucking hands off me!"

Jason stopped and grinned when he heard that voice. Jaclyn was here! Son of a bitch! He had been out there looking for her, hoping to get his hands on her, and Martin had her this whole time. That both excited and pissed him off.

Jason picked up his pace, rounded a corner, and collided with Jaclyn as she was trying to run away. He wrapped his arms tight around her body, and a smile spread across his face as his dick got hard.

"Hello, pretty girl," he said. "I've been looking for you.

"Jason!" The shock on her face was priceless. Clearly, she hadn't considered the possibility that they would ever bump into each other again.

Jason could tell by the dark circles under her eyes that they were drugging her. He didn't know what Martin wanted with Jaclyn, but he knew he had a few things he wanted to do. One was to give a little payback for the beatings he took in jail. Then, if there was anything left over, he might fuck her.

"Impressive, and yet disappointing." Josh Stan walked up to Jason, took hold of Jaclyn's arm, and yanked her away from Jason. "You were told to bring both. Twins are a rare thing with those animals and we wanted both." Josh glanced from the crying baby back up at Jason.

"She only had one," Jason answered, glaring at Josh, then licking his lips when his eyes went back to Jaclyn. She was stripped down and was wearing a dirty hospital gown. "How long has he had her?"

to be performed," Josh answered. "He's waiting for you." He moved to leave, but Jason stopped him.

"Where are you taking her?"

"Back to her cage." Josh sighed. "Clearly she needs another shot."

"Hold off on the drugs." Jason licked his lips again and reached out to touch her hair. "I want to play too." Jaclyn spit in his face and Jason quickly backhanded her, busting her lips open.

"That's enough," Josh snapped. He shoved Jaclyn into the hands of one of the free men behind Jason. "Put her back in the cage. You come with me," he said to Jason.

Jason followed Josh down another hallway to a door at the end. Josh didn't knock on the door, but opened it and went in. Martin had the room fixed up to resemble a very expensive office. There was a new tile floor, fresh white paint on the walls, leather chairs, and bookshelves all over the walls. The office looked nothing like the rest of the place that he'd seen so far.

"So you got only one," Martin said. He linked his hands over his chest and sat back in his chair. Josh also took a seat in a leather chair off to the side. "Disappointing, but considering that I gave you this task a few weeks ago and you did bring one, I'm a little impressed. You are proving to be very good at getting some things done."

Jason didn't say a thing.

"I also see that you met my other guest," Martin went on. He smiled when Jason frowned at him. "I see everything that goes on in my lab, Mr. Spencer. But I'm afraid that you can't play with her like you would wish. Ms. Davis has a very unique mark on her shoulder and I want all of my samples untouched, if you get my meaning."

Jason glared. "You knew I wanted her, damn it."

Martin tossed a thick envelope on his desk. When all Jason did was look at it, another one landed on top of it and two thick stacks of hundred dollar bills slipped out.

"One hundred thousand for the boy, Mr. Spencer," Martin stated. "And another hundred for your hands off the girl." When Jason tore his eyes from the money, Martin smiled.

Jason glared at the man. "I have some payback that needs to be done."

Martin glanced at Josh, who nodded. "You know, I think we can let him have a little bit of fun," Josh said, his eyes on Jason. "After all the drugs are interfering with the tests. Maybe a good beating will keep her clean and out long enough for the test I need."

Martin laughed. "You are a cold man, Josh." Jason looked from

Take your money, and you can have the girl for a few hours. Don't kill her, or have sex with her. I need our test subject to be untarnished, if you get my meaning."

Jason picked up the money. "I got you."

Martin sat forward in his chair and pressed a button. "Have the girl put into the room, and the kit ready for when she comes out." He released the button and sat back in his chair. "Have fun, Mr. Spencer."

Jason left the office with a huge smile on his face, a pocket full of cash, and knuckles itching to hit something. When he came back out to the lab, he stopped and looked around.

A steel table with thick leather straps was positioned in the middle of the room. What appeared to be a chemistry set and some other shit he didn't recognize were in the corners. The whole place had him thinking about something from a Frankenstein movie. In a cage was the kid, crying and screaming his head off and ignored by the small staff that was still setting things up.

Jason walked over to the cage and kicked it hard. "Shut the fuck up!" he yelled at the boy. "You don't understand this, but you're going to die. Your grandfather is going to come and cut you apart to see what's inside you, and I'm going to watch." He chuckled when the child's eyes got huge. Jason stood there, and for the hell of it kicked the cage once more. "Fucking freak."

He turned and started to whistle. One of the guys told him where Jaclyn was waiting for him. With a shit-eating grin on his face, he rubbed his hands together, and headed down to the locked room to have his fun. *Let the games begin.* He'd been waiting for this pay back for a long, long time.

Oh, he wasn't going to have sex with her. He did promise that. After all, she had been screwing an animal for God knew how long, and Jason didn't want any disease that she might be carrying. But he was going to mess her up *real* good.

"Damn that bitch can fight." One of the other guys who helped bring her in stopped Jason and handed him the key to the door. "The second her foot touched the ground, she kicked Brent in the nuts. You sure you don't want to give her something to calm her down a bit?"

Jason chuckled. "She was always good with her knees." He looked down at the key and recalled a time when he had cornered her. His hand had made it up her shirt to her belly before her knee landed in his nuts. Once he recovered, his father beat the hell out of him, because he wanted to touch her first. "And no, I don't want her drugged. I want her to feel everything I do to her."

up to the door. He put the key in, turned it, and walked into the room prepared for whatever might come at him.

    Jaclyn charged him, and Jason was ready. He turned to his right, blocking her hits with his arm, then swung around and backhanded her so hard that she went flying to the floor. Jason never did have a problem with hitting a woman and this one before him was a special treat. His first taste of beating a woman was when his father had let him beat on Lucy after Jaclyn left home. Then he had gotten the pleasure of nailing her.

    "Now, pretty girl." Jason closed the door carefully, wearing a cruel smile on his face. "Pretty girl" was the nickname he had always called her when she was still living at home, and she hated it. Jason locked the door, put the key in his pocket, then cracked his knuckles. "I have some unfinished business with you. And trust me, when I say it's going hurt you a hell of a lot more than it's going to hurt me."

Chapter Nine

Huddling in her cage, Jaclyn held her side in pain and tried to find a comfortable spot to sit but found none. She hurt like hell everywhere, thanks to the damn beating Jason just had to give her. Then, right after he was finished, they had dragged her out of the room and onto the table for their little damn test again. Apparently, the drugs they gave her to keep her calm and easy to deal with were messing up their samples. Well too damn bad!

She knew her face had to be a mess. She could feel the side swelling and knew her lip on the other side was split open, but what had her worried was if a rib or two might be broken. Sure as hell felt like it after the way he had kicked her. And to add insult to injury, she hurt between her legs where they scraped her womb until she started to bleed. Between her ribs and the cramping, Jaclyn wanted to die.

She knew that she shouldn't have left the house like a thief in the night, but she couldn't stay there. Not after the way Dedrick rejected her love and then made sure she understood that she was his for the taking. She loved him with all she had, but she couldn't stay with him if he didn't feel anything for her. And yet, here she was, in a cage waiting for the next torture to begin and wishing like hell that she could see Dedrick one last time.

Across the room in another cage, huddled over was Drake. Jaclyn could hear the sniffling as well as the coughing. Drake was sick, and being young in this dump, and with whatever shit Martin had up his sleeve, wasn't going to be good for him. The baby needed to be home, warm and safe in Sidney's arms, not here where these men treated him like he was some kind of animal.

It was a lab they were in, dark, quiet, and cold. Equipment lined the walls for the new experiments she didn't know anything about yet. Martin was planning something, because shit was coming and going in this place. But what had her shaking was when she was put back into her cage, she watched as they brought in a shock treatment machine. She only prayed that they didn't use it on Drake.

Lights flickered on, and the quiet was interrupted with the echoing footsteps coming down the hall. Jaclyn stiffened, waiting to see who and what was coming. Drake began to whimper again, and all Jaclyn could do was pray silently that he wasn't going to be hurt.

Conner Martin, Sidney's father, came out of the shadows and, bending over the cage where Drake was being held, just watched the baby. Jaclyn heard him talk to another guy who seemed to be cold and uncaring too, because he was nodding at whatever he was being told. Jaclyn started worrying when the guy standing next to Martin went over to the steel table and began to place syringes and sample dishes of different sizes on it. She couldn't take her eyes off of him as she watched him work with the shock treatment machine, flipping a switch and turning it on and bring tubes over to the table. "Oh God, help us! What are they planning to do now?"

"Blood and spinal both," Martin said, standing up. "Then we can get started on the brain. I also want stem cells."

"No!" Jaclyn came up to her knees, holding her side and wincing in pain. She watched in shock when they opened the cage, and yanked Drake out. He started screaming and kicking.

"Mamma!" Drake's little voice was so hoarse from his continuous screaming.

"Leave him alone!" Jaclyn cried. "He's just a baby!" Jason strode over and kicked her cage, which caused her to jump when more cramping hit. She closed her eyes as a trickle of blood ran down her leg.

Jason turned his cruel smile on her. "Shut the fuck up, bitch." He snickered. "Or I'm going to take you back into the room for round two."

"You can't do this." She tried once more to get their attention. Poor Drake was being pushed face down on the table, and then strapped into position. "He's your grandson!"

Jason kicked her cage again, but it was Martin who spoke to her. "No, Ms. Davis," he said calmly. "What this is, is an animal. Nothing more. And it's my job to protect humankind from the infections that have befallen my daughter."

Jaclyn pushed back the tears. "There is no infection," she said softly. "Your daughter fell in love."

"No!" Martin shouted. Drake screamed when the needle went into his arm, drawing out blood. Repeatedly he screamed for Sidney, and it broke Jaclyn's heart. "She was brainwashed, and as soon as I get rid of her infections then, she will come home and everything will be like it should be."

"You're out of your mind!" Jaclyn screeched in disbelief. She moved up on her knees, taking hold of one of the bars on the cage with one hand. "Nothing will ever be the same between you two. Do you think she'll forgive you after you torture her child?" Jason hit the cage again and Jaclyn lost her balance. She cried out in pain.

"This is no child," Martin yelled, his face getting red from anger. "It's an animal!"

"Mamma, Mamma, Mamma!" Drake screamed and panted on the table.

"At least give him something for the pain you shit-for-brains!" Jaclyn screamed at the guy who was about to stick a needle in Drake's back.

"Animals feel no pain," Martin snapped in anger.

He turned away from her and went over to the table. Jaclyn started to cry for Drake. He screamed at the top of his lungs when the needle went into his back and didn't stop until he passed out.

"You sick bastards!" Jaclyn sobbed.

It went on for hours. They tested and took from Drake until he passed out, only to wake him up and start the tests all over again. Pale and limp Drake was tossed back into the cage. Then she was brought out. It was her turn to be the guinea pig in their crazy experiments. The cramping only got worse as time passed. She was so weak, and her blood loss must be substantial. She heard Martin talking with the man she'd heard him with earlier, during her rest period. She overheard him saying he wanted fresh samples from Drake every six hours, and it made Jaclyn sick.

Jaclyn lost what little food she had in her stomach when they once again put Drake on the table and hooked wires to him. They brought the shock machine over, placed two wires on the side of his temple, and then turned it on. After they had shocked him three different times and took more samples, it was back into his cage. His little body was pale and bruised, and there wasn't a damn thing she could do to help him.

By morning, Martin was reading the test results and nodding his head in approval at something the man next to him was pointing out when a phone rang. Hope surged in Jaclyn when she heard that ring. Everyone stopped what they were doing and turned to Martin who pulled out the phone from his pocket. Jaclyn held her breath when he started smiling. She just had a gut feeling it was Sidney on the other end of this call.

"Hello, my dear," Martin said when he answered the phone. "I was wondering how long it was going to take you to come to your senses and call."

It *was* Sidney. Jaclyn crawled on her knees to the door of the cage. Her full attention was on the one-sided conversation. She prayed that Sidney would be able to talk some sanity into her father. She pushed the pain in her body, the cramps and bleeding aside in order to hear the one side of the conversation.

"Why, yes." Martin turned and still smiling glanced at Jaclyn. "I have her right here. I must say, Sidney, I'm disappointed that you would socialize with trash like this. That girl doesn't fit in with our family, but she is making a great test subject."

Jaclyn gave Martin a dirty look before he turned back around, giving Jaclyn his back.

"See, pretty girl? You belong with me. No one else can appreciate you the way I do." Jason snickered and walked around the cage dragging his fingers across each bar of the cage. "I'm the one who knows you best."

Jaclyn ignored him and strained to catch every word Martin was saying on the phone.

"No, I'm sorry, Sidney." Martin's voice changed in tone. The sweet voice he had been using with Sidney rapidly changed to a cold and harsh one. "That *thing* is not your child. It's an animal!"

"You're never going to get out of here." Jason was amused by all of this. She heard the happiness in his voice, could tell that he was enjoying it. "And just so you know, when the old man is finished with you, I get what's left."

Jaclyn snorted. "What are you going to do?" She turned and sneered back at him. "Talk me to death, because I doubt if you can do anything to me with that thing you try to call a penis." His face turned red, and Jaclyn laughed. "Remember, Jason. I walked in on you while you were in the bathroom. I saw what you had between your legs, and it was short of…impressive."

Jason kicked the cage and it knocked Jaclyn to the floor. "Keep up the smart mouth, bitch, and I'm going to show just *what* I can do with my dick."

"You're going to have to forgive me, my dear," Martin said, drawing her attention away from Jason. "But I'm going to have to go. I need to do another round of tests before I call it a night." He hung the cell phone up, giving Jaclyn an emotionless glance. "Mr. Spencer, it's time for you to go to your new job." His cold eyes fixed on Jaclyn. "And you, my dear, have another test to participate in."

* * * *

"Got it!" Adrian called out once Sidney dropped the phone and broke down in Stefan's arms. "You son of a bitch," he said through gritted teeth. "Same fucking place as Jaclyn's cell phone signal."

"Stefan, I feel his pain," Sidney whispered. "How is it possible for me to feel it?"

eye and understood. The boys were still linked with Sidney since she was still breast-feeding, so anything bad that happened to them she was going to feel. It was almost as if they were still attached to her womb.

"What do we do?" Adrian asked.

Dedrick tore his eyes from his brother and wife and looked back down at Adrian. "I guess you get to blow shit up."

"Sweet." Adrian smiled, rubbing his hands together. "Just give me twenty, and I'll have what I need ready."

"You're just determined to get him blown up." Skyler rolled her eyes and followed Adrian out of the office.

"You know a big bang is just what we need," Stefan stated. He was still holding Sidney tight with Brock on her lap crying still. "Rock their world a bit."

Dedrick couldn't stop the grin spreading across his lips. "I'm starting to like the twisted side of Adrian."

"I put a call in for Doctor Sager." Natasha came into the room and tried to take Brock, but he wouldn't let go of Sidney. "She's going to meet you at the hospital. She has rooms already for Drake and Jaclyn."

"You think they're in bad shape?" Dedrick couldn't shake the dreaded feeling.

"I don't want to take the chance," Natasha said. "If they're sick or worse, the hospital is the best place to handle whatever has been done to them. The doctor is also making a call for a few guards of our kind to be there in case more trouble comes." She knelt and touched Brock's head. "This is personal, boys, and I've never asked you to do anything that may harm others." Natasha looked up at both Stefan and Dedrick. "Tonight, I don't care what you have to do. Just bring them home."

Dedrick didn't mince words. "Then I want Dad's shot gun."

Natasha caught his eye and slowly stood up. "Follow me."

* * * *

They forced Jaclyn back into her cage once more. Sweat covered her from head to toe, and pain pounded at every inch of her body. Plus, she was bleeding all down her legs, thanks to them scraping her uterus raw.

They had strapped her down on the table, stripped her, and placed her legs up in stirrups. A leather strap was belted around her mouth to help muffle her screams when they gave her a pelvic examination, without any of the drugs she had previously been given. Her vagina had been scraped, and then blood had been taken from both of her arms. She screamed and cried from the pain they inflicted while they probed between her legs, and it seemed as though they had taken samples from

When they started, there had been a little bleeding from the earlier testing, but now, she was flowing heavy. All she could do was lie on the cold floor of her cage, pant from the pain, and pray for death. They had even taken a razor blade and scraped skin from the mark on her shoulder, making it bleed, too.

She tried to stay awake for Drake, with the hope to reassure him by her presence. Jaclyn wasn't close enough to tell if he was sleeping or if he had passed out cold from all the "tests" Martin insisted on performing. Her bleeding wasn't stopping, and it was making her so weak. Her eyes closed, the sounds around her were muffled, but she couldn't get her body to let go completely. She just drifted in and out of awareness.

Jaclyn cried out when the cramps hit her hard in the stomach. Tears slipped from her eyes from the throbbing pain, and she could feel a fresh wave of blood pour out of her. When she got the strength to open her eyes she started to cry. The pain was almost unbearable, and she knew without a doubt she was dying.

Boom!

Everything and everyone stopped. Jaclyn found the strength to rise on her arms and look around the room but saw nothing. She was panting through the pain. Her life felt like it was slipping away with the blood draining out of her body.

"What was that?" someone asked.

"Who gives a shit?" another answered. "We need to get another sample from that kid or it's our asses.

Boom! This time things shook when another explosion went off. Jaclyn dropped back down and she cried out. There were only five men left to finish the tests, and they were all walking to the center of the room. She managed to see a thick cloud of smoke coming from one of the dark hallways into the large clearing, but she was too weak to make anything out of it.

She thought she was dreaming when she heard heavy footsteps. It wasn't possible when out of the smoke, she saw the outline of thick legs in black jeans, a narrow waist, a wide chest, and even thicker arms. Jaclyn lost her breath when her eyes landed on the face of Dedrick, and she shook her head to stop herself from passing out. Even though he seemed pissed, with his eyes red and his lips thinned out, he was a sight sent from heaven with his arm up on his shoulder, holding something.

"Dedrick." Jaclyn breathed out before the pain and darkness took her.

* * * *

something that belongs to me." Dedrick pulled the double-barrel shotgun off his shoulder. He took aim and shot one guy then another. "And I want her back, motherfuckers," he growled.

Stefan made his way up next to Dedrick and shot two more before looking at Dedrick and shaking his head. "You just couldn't wait, could you?"

"And you two can never pay attention to shit," Adrian said. Both turned around and Adrian was standing with another guy in a head lock. One hard twist and he broke the guy's neck. Adrian shook his head at both of them. "Can we hurry it up, please? Those explosives are on a five-minute timer."

"Drake!" Stefan yelled.

Stefan went looking for Drake and Adrian went to work at trashing the lab. Dedrick ran his eyes around the room trying to find any evidence of Jaclyn or Drake when he spotted a puddle of blood on the floor. When he followed the trail it led him right to the cage where Jaclyn lay, sprawled inside and wearing a dirty gown with a large pool of blood between her legs.

"No!" Dedrick cried out. He dropped the gun next to the cage door and with all his might pulled until he broke the lock and opened the door. He grabbed hold of her limp body, dragged her out, and draped her across his lap. Her head rolled back. "No, no, no," he pleaded. "Jaclyn, please God, don't leave me." He searched for a pulse and breathed a sigh of relief when he found one, but the sight of her beaten face and the blood coming from between her legs had him fearing that she might die very soon if he didn't get her to the hospital. "Adrian, I need a blanket!"

Dedrick touched her face and felt tears coming to his eyes. "Don't you give up now, damn it!"

"Shit." Adrian gasped, putting the blanket around her body. "We need to get her to the hospital."

"He tortured him," Stefan said, his voice hollow. "Look at my boy!"

Adrian hung the phone up, picked up the shotgun, and peeked at his watch. "We *have* to go. Now!"

Dedrick scooped Jaclyn up in his arms and followed Adrian and Stefan out. He glanced back behind him, and fear gripped him when he saw that with each step they took there was a trail of blood following.

"You're going to be all right," Dedrick whispered, shifting her so her head rested on his shoulder. "Do you hear me? You know how stubborn I am, so you listen and listen good, Jaclyn Davis. You leave follow you and bend you over my knee."

Adrian opened the door for both Stefan and Dedrick. As soon as the doors closed, he was speeding away toward the hospital. The three of them didn't even look back when the building exploded.

* * * *

"She has two cracked ribs on her left side and four bruised ones on the right." Doctor Sager stood in front of Dedrick outside Jaclyn's room, her arms crossed over her chest and concern all over her face. Since Jaclyn was bleeding, she had checked on her first and let her assistant check on Drake.

"But that isn't why she was bleeding so heavy," Dedrick said.

"No." Dr. Sager took a deep breath and looked down at the floor.

"Doc?" Dedrick got scared. He didn't like the way the doctor was acting and was starting to fear the worst.

"I'm sorry, Mr. Draeger." Dr. Sager gave him a sad grimace. "Your mate miscarried a baby." Dedrick's jaw dropped. "The drugs that were pumped into her system, the beating and whatever else was done to her caused her to miscarry."

Dedrick thought he was going to pass out. He swayed on his feet. She reached out to grab him, but he ended up going down to the floor anyway. "How…how far along?" he asked, tears falling down his face.

"About four weeks," she answered.

Four weeks. He added it up in his brain. Four weeks ago was when he had sex with her the first time in the pool house. "Oh God!" he moaned, covering his face with his hands.

"I'm very worried about her uterus," Dr. Sager went on. "They have taken a good amount of the lining away, and she is going to have a lot of scarring. I won't lie, but I can't be certain if your mate will ever be able to have children. I don't know what they did to her, and I don't think I want to know. She's going to be in a lot of pain for the next few days, and I'm keeping her here in the hospital to watch her carefully. She's lost a lot of blood."

"Does she know?"

"Yes," Dr. Sager answered. "I've had to sedate her, so you might want to wait until the morning to see her."

Dedrick nodded, and Dr. Sager left him there on the floor. A baby. That bastard took a child from him before it even had a chance at life. How was he going to keep the rage down now?

"Dedrick?" Natasha came over to him and knelt down. "Are you all right?" Her voice was gentle and caring.

"She lost a baby," Dedrick said, staring straight ahead at the wall in front of him, tears falling freely. "She was pregnant, and we didn't even know it, and now it's gone."

"Oh." Natasha covered her mouth with her hand. "I'm so sorry."

"The doc doesn't know if she'll ever be able to have kids now." He was numb, and his voice sounded hollow. "And it's all my fault."

"None of this is your fault," Natasha said, touching his head. "You didn't cause her to lose the baby or for that man to do the things he did."

Dedrick nodded. "Yes I did. I pushed her away." He turned to his mother. "She told me she loved me, and I told her I didn't love her." Fresh tears fell. "I lied to her, Ma. I lied because I was scared of loving a human. Scared shitless of hurting her physically."

"It's natural to be scared," Natasha said. "You have enough human DNA in you to make human mistakes, and that was what this was. A mistake. And loving someone doesn't go away because of loss or anger. I'm sure Jaclyn still loves you, even if she wants to rip your head off."

Dedrick smiled. "How can she forgive me now when I can't forgive myself?"

"Because she loves you." Sidney stood in front of him and smiled. She knelt, touched his face, and before Dedrick could brace himself, she hugged him. "Thank you," she whispered. "You saved my son. Now save my best friend." Sidney kissed him on the cheek before she let him go and left.

Dedrick smiled. "That's one hell of a woman my brother married."

Natasha smiled also. "Yes it is. And there is another hell of a woman in that room waiting for you." She stood up and brushed her slacks off. "Don't screw it up, or I'll have your ass this time."

Dedrick also stood up. "Yes, ma'am." Stefan came out of the room next to Jaclyn, looking about as somber as Dedrick felt. "How's Drake?"

Stefan shoved his hands into his pockets. "I've never wanted to take another life as much as I want to take Conner Martin's. The bastard took spinal fluid, blood, stem cells for Christ sakes," he hissed, running a hand over his face and into his hair. "And the best one for last. He shocked Drake's brain, then took spinal fluid from the back of his neck. Who the hell does that to a little boy?"

"A sick bastard," Dedrick answered. He also took a deep breath and shoved his hands into his pockets. "Jaclyn lost a baby."

"Oh man!" Stefan groaned.

"Something big is about to happen, Stefan," Dedrick said. "I can from a kid unless you have plans for it."

"Let's hope like hell we destroyed all the samples."

* * * *

Conner Martin sat in the back seat of his car. Rain was pouring down outside as he waited for the scientist he'd hired to show. He wanted results. After the building had been blown up and all his samples but the one he'd taken with him had been lost, Martin wasn't a very happy man. His work wasn't progressing the way he believed it should. Too many interruptions by those things his daughter associated with.

He glanced at his watch. The impatience was wearing on him. He wasn't the kind of man who liked to be kept waiting for too long, and that was just what this man was doing. Making him wait.

Martin was about to tell his driver to leave when bright headlights flashed. *He's here!* Martin smiled and waited for the man to come to him. After all Martin was paying him nicely for his services.

"You're late," Martin said as soon as the man was in the car. "And my time is money, Doctor."

"And that's why I'm late." The scientist in the dark suit pulled his briefcase onto his lap, opened it, and handed a file to Martin. "I wanted to bring you the good news."

Martin got excited but didn't let it show. He opened the file and quickly read over the notes. When he looked up at the man, the doctor smiled and nodded.

"A perfect specimen. It took, and as soon as the cage is ready and the lab is set up, I'll grow it."

"And it split I see." Martin read some more. "What are you going to do with the second?"

"Freeze it." The doctor closed his case. "Unless I need it for something else. That one is male, the other female. I'll let you know as soon as the growth is starting."

Martin smiled. "I look forward to your report."

Chapter Ten
One month later...

"I don't see why you think you have to leave now," Sidney whined to Jaclyn, who was packing what few belongings she had, leaving everything that Natasha and Skyler had bought her once again. "Your ribs are still bothering you."

"It's time," Jaclyn said, coming out of the bathroom with her makeup and brushes. Refusing to look at Sidney, she dumped them into her bag. If she looked, then Sid would guilt her into staying even longer. Already, she'd been here two more weeks than she had originally agreed to or wanted to be.

"You need to talk to him."

Jaclyn stopped what she was doing for a split second. "No I don't." She went back into the bathroom and came out with her straightener.

"It doesn't stop because you want it to." Sidney leaned over the bag, her face in front of Jaclyn. "Jacy, you need to talk to him."

"I can't," Jaclyn whispered. She pushed away from her backpack and sat down at the foot of the bed. "I can't open myself up like that again, Sid. He broke my heart, and right now, I don't have much of it left." She kicked her foot out. "And the baby thing still bothers me."

Jaclyn sat there, and her hand went up to her shoulder, rubbing the mark that was still there. Every time she thought about Dedrick she would touch the spot and burn for him. After she had gotten out of the hospital, the family had brought her here to finish healing. She had felt very uncomfortable staying here and even worse when Dedrick had ended up carrying her to her bed. She was very depressed over the miscarriage and didn't want to see anyone. Sidney was the only one she allowed in the room, but that was because she refused to leave. Jaclyn supposed it was a good thing. She needed that shoulder to cry on, and she did a lot of crying.

Drake was still traumatized, and Jaclyn didn't blame him. What they'd done to that poor baby was so unbelievable, it would be a long time before he felt safe again. He hung on Sidney like a second layer of skin. Sid told her he had bronchitis, and it had progressed into pneumonia. He had been put on strong antibiotics, and he was kept in intensive care for treatment, until all chances of any further infections had passed. The doctors released him to come home a couple of weeks after Jaclyn. The shock treatments to his brain though had everyone worried. They didn't know what kind of damage might have occurred and wouldn't know until he got older, but because he was so young, they hoped his brain would regenerate itself and protect him from any lasting damage.

Jaclyn shook off the past and stood up. She quickly closed her bag. "I've got to go."

She rushed out of the room and was halfway down the stairs when she saw Natasha. "Are you sure you want to leave?"

Jaclyn smiled and nodded. "I have to. Thanks for letting me stay. I think this is one of the few places I've ever been that I can call home."

"Honey, you're welcome to stay here anytime." Natasha pulled her into her arms, hugging her tightly. "You are family to me. Never forget that," she whispered.

Jaclyn closed her eyes and accepted the embrace. It pained her to be walking away from this home and the people that she cared about, but she had to. It was all comforting but more than that, it was way too painful.

Slowly, she pulled out of Natasha's arms and, with her head lowered, continued down the stairs. Jaclyn stopped when she saw the boots that belonged only to Dedrick. She took a deep breath and raised her eyes to him.

After all this time, he still looked damn good to her. Jeans that seemed like they were so tight they were going to split if he moved. T-shirt tucked into the waistband, the outline of his stomach showing, and those damn arms of his. God, how she wanted them wrapped around her each and every night of her life, but knew it would never happen. Just staring at him now, she could hear him telling her how he didn't love her and wasn't falling in love either.

Time seemed to stand still. Their eyes locked, but neither said a word. Jaclyn wanted so much to spill her heart out to him and tell him all the things she wanted. But it wouldn't do any good, and she knew it. Dedrick made it very clear to her where they stood.

"Take care of yourself, Dedrick," she finally said. "That's what you seem to be good at." She moved around him toward the door, and his voice stopped her.

"Don't go," he said. Jaclyn didn't turn around but waited to see if he would say anything else. "Please."

"Why?" She couldn't meet him in the eye, knew if she did then she was going to break down and cry, and the hell if she was going to put herself out there again to be hurt.

"Jaclyn, look at me."

Jaclyn took a deep breath, willed the tears away, and swung around to face him. "What, Dedrick?" she demanded. "You want to stomp on me one more time?"

"Stay." He said the word so softly that she thought she hadn't heard him right.

"What?" She frowned.

"Stay." He took two steps closer. "I'm asking you to stay here and be a part of the family." He licked his lips. Jaclyn had never seen Dedrick acting so nervous like he was right now. "Me and you." He moved his hand as he talked. "We're heading toward something that I've never in my life thought was possible, because you are human. And I know I've tossed that at you several times." He spoke in a hurry before she could interrupt him. "But it's true, Jacy. It never crossed my mind that I could care for anyone besides the members of my family. I held onto the hope of finding my mate, but not having any real feelings for her." He took another step closer. "Does that make any sense to you at all?"

"No." Jaclyn sighed.

He took a deep breath. "I'm scared, Jacy. There is so much I'm afraid of right now. I don't even know where to begin, to even try to share with you. There's one thing keeping me up late at night, though. If you walk out that door, will I ever see you again?" Another step closer. "I can't lose you. Not after it took me so long to find you." Another step, and he was standing so close that she could smell him and feel his body heat. "Stay with me." He touched her cheek, and she closed her eyes. "You're my mate, my lady, my heart, and soul. My love."

"You shit," she whispered, a tear slipping free.

"I asked you once what you wanted. Now I'm going to tell you what I want." He brushed her hair, and she opened her eyes. "I want you in my bed each morning kissing me awake. I want you to be in my arms at night fulfilling each and every fantasy I have just like I know you want me to do for you. I want you always to need me like I need you now." He smiled shyly. "I even want your smart-ass mouth telling me what I should or shouldn't be doing."

Jaclyn couldn't believe it. Dedrick was opening up to her, and she didn't know what to do or say. All she could do was stand there and let him talk.

"Say something, please."

Jaclyn couldn't say anything, but she decided to do one even better. She grabbed the front of his shirt and yanked him down, kissing him deep. Dedrick moaned and wrapped his arms around her, picking her around.

"Ah shit!" Stefan groaned. "He did it here?"

"That's fifty you owe me." Adrian smiled.

Jaclyn looked over at Stefan and Adrian who just came out of the front room. Adrian had one arm over Stefan's shoulder with his hand out. Stefan was digging into his pocket and slapped a fifty into his hand.

"You bet on this?" Jaclyn asked.

Adrian shrugged. "Only on where he was going to do it. Stefan said he would catch you outside. I said before you reached the door."

"Adrian," Dedrick said.

"Yes?" Adrian smiled.

"Now I'm going to kick your ass." Dedrick let go of Jaclyn and ran after Adrian, who took off into the family room.

"Welcome to the family." Natasha sighed, wrapping her arm around Jaclyn's waist. "It's one crazy household."

* * * *

It was after midnight. Jaclyn was standing under the hot spray of Dedrick's shower, which, all things considered, she guessed it was hers now as well. She closed her eyes while the water beat down over her head. It had turned out to be one hell of a day, one she never thought would end the way it had. Finally, she had Dedrick in love with her, and it felt great.

She pulled her long hair over to her left shoulder, turned the knob hotter, then hung her head, and braced her hands on the wall. Jaclyn sighed at the extra heat that beat down on her sore body. After she agreed to stay, damn if Dedrick didn't shock the hell out of her even more by proposing. Then, the entire family went out to dinner for a small celebration. The meal turned out to be long, but so much fun.

After they came home Stefan and Adrian dragged Dedrick off, and she went to help Sidney with the boys. Natasha and Skyler moved her things from the guest room to Dedrick's so fast that she didn't know what was going on. Then, when she thought the night couldn't get longer, Skyler decided to shock everyone with her good news and announce she was pregnant. Jaclyn shook her head and smiled at the memory of Adrian going white, then whooping it up around the house like a child hollering in happiness.

"Ah, you started without me," Dedrick moaned.

Jaclyn turned and watched him strip down through the glass before he opened the shower door and stepped in. She felt his body brushing up against her back and had to sway her hips to tease him, just a little pressing against her, his arms resting next to hers, hands flat on the wall and his erection resting beside the slit of her pussy, teasing her.

"You know, we haven't fooled around in the shower yet," he said in her ear before he sucked the lobe into his mouth. "Care to start indulging in my fantasies, mate?"

She smiled when he moved his hands down her arms and skimmed them up under, cupping her breasts. Jaclyn sucked the air into her lungs sharply from the contact. Squeezing her breasts, he kneaded the mounds and brushed his thumbs across her tight nipples. The head of his cock bumped against her clit, and once again, she hung her head and moaned while pushing back against him.

"Are you trying to tease me?" She moved her hips back and forth to tease the cock that was seeking entrance to her body. Jaclyn inhaled sharply when the head of his cock slid over her clit, and then moved on to her entrance, nudging to get in. "Shit," she moaned.

"You want something, baby?" he cooed. "Because I think I have something you might be interested in."

In her experience, no one else had ever teased her in the shower with so little touching and yet had her burning up for so much more of the same. In the past, they would walk in, maybe wash her body, do some kissing and touching, and then it was off with the water and into the bed. But Dedrick was different. He touched her in a way that always had her wanting more and never wanting it to end. Like now, he was cupping her breasts and teasing her with his cock, but it was enough to have her ready to toss him on the shower floor and ride him until they both were hoarse from screaming.

Dedrick moved his right arm around her chest, took hold of her left breast, and skimmed his left hand down her stomach to her mound. He moved her left leg, spreading her, and then touched her clit. The contact had her jumping and arching back, which helped his cock to slip farther inside. But Dedrick held it all back from her, taking out what little had slid in so the head was all that remained.

Jaclyn reached behind her, fisting both hands into his wet hair. Together they lowered themselves to the floor of the shower on their knees, and with that movement Dedrick's cock pushed into her. She was filled and stretched with the width of his flesh, and God help her, she did love it almost as much as she loved him.

Holding onto his hair, Jaclyn moved up and down on the length of him. She didn't move fast, just slow and easy, dragging out each sensation, each feeling. Dedrick kissed and sucked on her neck. His hands moved back to her breasts, squeezing and pinching the nipples between his fingers.

They didn't talk. Words weren't needed and Jaclyn didn't think she would be able to form a word anyhow with the pleasure she was feeling at the moment.

"Ah, shit baby," Dedrick moaned. "You feel so damn good."

Jaclyn loved the slow and easy, but she also needed him harder and faster. So she moved her hands back to the wall and pushed herself down on his cock powerfully. Dedrick moaned and moved his hands from her breasts over to her hips. He helped her slam down on his flesh, and with each slap, she reached closer for her pleasure.

Her head hung down, and she thrust her hips as fast and as she could. Dedrick growled behind her and it fueled her. She loved hearing him coming unglued just like she loved feeling his pleasure inside her.

"Yeah, mate." He groaned. "Ride it. Take it all!"

Jaclyn screamed and climaxed, but Dedrick forced her to ride it out. He stayed on his knees but shifted her a little so she was more on her hands and knees and not leaning against the wall. He thrust into her hard, which rocked her right into another orgasm.

"I'm coming!" he yelled behind her, then his mouth closed down on her shoulder, and he bit her. Jaclyn moaned and closed her eyes.

They stayed in the shower until the hot water turned cold. Jaclyn couldn't stop kissing him or touching him, and even ended up sucking his cock until he came again. She barely got dried off after the shower before Dedrick was picking her up and loving her body again.

The clock on the nightstand read three in the morning, but Jaclyn still wasn't ready to let all the memories go so she could relax into sleep. She couldn't stop smiling. After all this time, she finally had his arms wrapped tightly around her body, just like in her dreams, and she didn't want to sleep and miss a moment of these comfortable feelings.

They were lying naked, stretched out on sheets on the floor, with her back against his chest, and their bodies were damp from another round of who-is-going-to-be-on-top. She'd won.

"I think I can hear the smile on your face," Dedrick said, tightening his arms around her. He moved then onto the bed and looked down at her, chuckled then dropped his head back down on the pillow. "Why are you smiling?"

"Because your arms are finally wrapped around me." She sighed. "And I love it."

"Well, I love you," he whispered. "Now go to sleep before I roll you over and take my turn at being on top."

She snuggled back against him and closed her eyes to go to sleep, asleep?"

"I was." He sighed. "Do you need more loving, woman?"

She kissed his arm. "No. I want to ask you something."

"Ask away then." He shifted in the bed, rubbing his body against her backside as if he was a cat.

"Do you think we will ever have kids?" He didn't answer her, so Jaclyn turned over in the bed, coming face-to-face with him. "You don't, do you?"

He gave her a smile. "Yeah, I think we will have kids. I just don't know how long it will take. You got pregnant once, so I think you will again."

She leaned in and kissed him before pushing him onto his back and coming over him. "Then I think we should get started at making that baby."

Dedrick grinned with an eyebrow going up. "You on top?"

Jaclyn took hold of his wrists and pinned them over his head. "Yeah, me on top. Got a problem with that?"

Dedrick moved and changed their positions, pinning her under him with *her* wrists over her head. "As a matter of fact I do, mate. It's my turn to be on top."

Jaclyn wrapped her legs around his waist. "Then get to riding, baby. I'm still hungry."

Dedrick laughed, leaned down, and kissed her deep. Not giving her any kind of warning, he thrust hard, embedding his cock to the max inside her, and Jaclyn instantly came.

Chapter Eleven
Ten years later...

"Ow!" Jaclyn moaned, squeezing Dedrick's hand while he rubbed her back, waiting for the contraction to subside. "Have I told you that I hate your fucking guts?" She groaned.

Dedrick smirked. "A few times now."

Ten years. It took them ten years before nature decided to let them have a child, and Dedrick was thrilled. It had been a hard pregnancy for Jaclyn. She started having trouble almost from the beginning. By her fourth month, she was put on light bed rest. She was bleeding and having cramps. Because she was human, the doctor didn't want to take any unnecessary chances for her to miscarry. Dedrick was informed that Jaclyn was to stay off her feet. That seemed to help until her sixth month. Then, her body wanted to start labor, and the birth canal began to dilate. She was given medicine to stop the labor, and she was put to bed for good. When she needed to use the restroom for anything, Dedrick carried her. He even bathed her, which took a huge toll on his sanity. Even large with his child, Jaclyn was damn hot and made him walk around for hours with a stiff dick.

"I need something," Jaclyn cried. She sounded so broken and so tired that it was killing him. He wished like hell that he could take her pain away, but this was something that he couldn't do for her.

"The nurse called, and they'll be up with your epidural any time," Dedrick tried to soothe her but figured it wasn't working too well.

"God," she groaned. "I don't know how the hell Sidney did this with those boys." She squeezed his hand and yelled, then broke down. "I can't do this. It hurts too much."

Dedrick waited for the contraction to slip away before he straightened up. "I'm going to go look for the nurse." He moved over to the door, nodded to Sidney to go in, then jogged to the nurse's station. "Um, yeah, hello. My wife needs that epidural."

"Mr. Draeger, they're in another room, and she's next." The nurse smiled.

Dedrick nodded and went back over to Stefan. Feeling more tired and tense than he ever had in his life, he rolled his shoulders and popped his neck.

"How is she?" Stefan asked.

"Hurting," Dedrick answered. He rubbed his face and groaned. "Shit Stefan, I don't think I can watch this. It's killing me to see her in so much pain."

placed his hand on Dedrick's shoulder. "She'll be fine."

Dedrick understood that Stefan was trying to comfort him, but it wasn't working. He glanced around the area. "Where's Mom and Adrian?" he asked when all he saw in the small waiting area were Skyler and her three children. For ten years, Skyler and Adrian were having kids left and right. Already, his baby sister was expecting her fourth child.

"The boys were with Adrian, and he came back without them. Said he lost them, somewhere so she went with him to help find them." Stefan chuckled. "I do *not* want to be them when Sidney gets a hold of them. She is so pissed that Adrian lost them in a hospital, and I was going to go after them, but Mom told me to stay here in case you freaked out." He turned to Dedrick, giving him the once over. "It never fails. Mom is right. You do look like you're about to freak out."

"I don't remember you being so calm when the boys were born," Dedrick snapped back.

"Stefan!" Natasha came at a fast pace down the hall holding onto one arm of each boy looking so pissed that Stefan and Dedrick took a step back. Dedrick had only seen his mother that angry once—the night he had been brought home by the police. "Where is Sidney?"

"In with Jaclyn." Stefan frowned, but Dedrick knew what was going on. The twins were a handful, one that only their mother seemed to be able to handle. It amazed Dedrick that Sidney could control those two the way Natasha seemed to be able to control them through the years. "What did these two do now?"

"You wouldn't believe it." Natasha huffed.

"But I bet I would." Sidney came out of the room and Dedrick didn't think he'd ever seen her so pissed at the boys in their young lives. He might not have seen her this angry since she had been mated to his brother. "Jaclyn is getting her epidural," she said to Dedrick, then turned back to the twins. Dedrick had to put his hand over his mouth to hide his smile. Sidney reminded him of his mother when Stefan used to get in trouble. "I'm going to take a guess here." She tapped her finger on her lips as if she was thinking. "Playing doctor or wheelchair racing?"

"It was him." Both boys pointed to the other as Natasha held onto their arms.

"Right." Sidney walked up to them, took hold of an ear on each of them, and marched them over to the waiting area without another word.

Dedrick chuckled. "They act like you," he said to Stefan. He placed his hand on Stefan's shoulder, just like Stefan had him. "I'm

Good luck with them."

Dedrick opened the room door smiling at the anesthesiologist who was packing up. Jaclyn was lying back on the bed, her eyes closed. A nurse was checking her. To him, Jaclyn looked like she was glowing. These past nine months had been torture on him with not being able to help her or take any of this suffering away for her.

"Feeling better?" he asked, easing down on the bed and taking Jaclyn's hand.

"I'm tired," she answered before taking a deep breath and letting it out slowly.

Dedrick grinned when she pulled his arm closer, forcing him to lie down behind her in the small bed and wrap his arms around her. It was one of those things she loved, and he had to do it every night. Wrap his arms around her body and hold her through the night. It was a tough job, but someone had to do it. God knew how happy he was to be the one chosen for the duty.

Dedrick rubbed her large belly. He was reminded with a kick that soon his child would be in this world. A child that he hadn't even realized he had wanted until Jaclyn came into his world and woken him from a dead sleep.

"So you want to bet now on if it's a boy or a girl?" he asked.

Since the first sonogram, they had been trying to discover the sex of their child and each time they tried, the baby turned from them. The doctor thought it was funny, pointing out to Jaclyn that each shifter child has a special link to its mother, could pick up the mother's thoughts. A special gift that gradually went away as the children grew up. The doctor was pretty sure that this child knew that they wanted to know what it was, and it was turning away on purpose.

"You want a boy," Jaclyn said. She was so tired it showed in her voice. "I've known that for months."

Dedrick brushed her hair away from her face and kissed her neck. "And what would you say if I told you I want a girl?"

Jaclyn stiffened in his arms and groaned. "I just want it over," she cried. "Something's wrong."

Dedrick felt his heart drop at those two words she moaned out. He got off the bed, moved the sheet, and looked between her legs. Blood was on the pad under her.

Dedrick didn't waste a moment telling Jaclyn anything. He ran from the room, almost knocked Stefan over, and collided with Dr. Sager, who was reading a file. "She...she...Jaclyn," he stuttered. "Blood...there's blood."

a nurse and rushed with Dedrick back into the room. When they opened the door, Jaclyn was sitting up crying, pale and clearly in pain again. Dedrick felt helpless standing there watching while the doctor checked Jaclyn's cervix and a nurse was trying to calm her down.

"Mr. Draeger, we need to do an emergency C-section," the doctor told Dedrick. "Right now!"

"Wh…wh…why?" He was scared shitless and feeling like he was about to pass out from the way everyone in the room was moving in rapid motion. He tried not to cry, but there was no way in hell he could stop the tears from falling. There was only one other time in his life that he had been this scared, and Dedrick hated when he recalled the night he found Jaclyn in that room bleeding. "What's wrong?"

"The placenta has ruptured. If we don't get the baby out, your wife could bleed to death, and the baby will die." The doctor looked at the nurse. "Let's go!"

Dedrick was pushed out of the room with the bed, but once in the hall he could only stand there as Jaclyn was wheeled away to the operating room. He was stunned. Everything was going fine, or so he thought. Her labor was progressing just the way it should, and in the blink of an eye, everything changed.

"Dedrick?" Sidney touched his arm, and in a daze, he stared down at her hand. "What's happening?"

Dedrick snapped out of his daze and looked back down the hall. "They're taking her for a C-section. I…I've got to go."

Shaking off the uneasy feeling, Dedrick took off at a jog down the hall. He skidded to a halt at a set of double doors just as a nurse in scrubs was coming out.

"Mr. Draeger, please put these on. Then you can join your wife."

Dedrick didn't know he could dress so fast. When he was done, the nurse led him into the operating room where Jaclyn was already strapped down. He was taken to a stool next to her head, and he immediately took her hand. "Hey."

Jaclyn squeezed his hand and a tear slipped down her cheek. "Boy." She swallowed hard. "Only a son of yours could give us this much trouble."

Dedrick chuckled and kissed her forehead. "I think a girl like you would be my next pain in the ass."

Jaclyn started to laugh, but seemed to think better of it. "I'm scared," she whispered.

"Me too."

Time seemed to stand still for him as he waited for his child.

Jaclyn, but it was hard when his mind kept thinking about the bad shit. He couldn't lose her. If he did, Dedrick knew that he would die.

"All right you two," the doctor said. "I'm reaching in for the head." Dedrick squeezed Jaclyn's hand and smiled. "We have a baby!"

Dedrick let the air he was holding out in a rush the second he heard the loud cry. He turned quickly as the baby was held up for them both to see.

"How does a girl sound to you two?" Dr. Sager said before handing the screaming baby off to a nurse to clean up.

"A girl!" he said softy and leaned over to give Jaclyn a gentle kiss.

Jaclyn smiled dreamily.

Dedrick turned around to the nurse who was standing there with a bundle in her arms. A bundle that was still crying loudly.

"Mr. Draeger." She handed Dedrick the baby. "Say hello to your daughter."

Dedrick took his little girl in his arms and tears fell from his eyes. "Oh, Jacy, she's perfect."

A daughter. A cherished little girl who was already wrapping her daddy around that tiny finger of hers. He couldn't speak. He was mesmerized by the face of his angel.

"She's perfect," Dedrick said again. He tore his eyes from the baby to smile at Jaclyn who was smiling right back at him. "You've given me the most precious gift." He kissed Jaclyn again before he leaned the baby in so Jaclyn could kiss her. "Thank you."

"Mr. Draeger. Would you like to carry her down to the nursery?"

Dedrick glanced at the nurse then at Jaclyn, who nodded. "Go. I'm fine now."

Dedrick stood up with the baby and left, following the nurses to the nursery, where his daughter was taken from his arms and placed under a warming light. He watched while she was checked over from head to toe, still not believing his eyes. Dedrick knew that he should go out and tell the family that they had a little girl and that Jaclyn was now doing fine, but he couldn't seem to pull himself away from the tiny infant. He thought he was happy with Jaclyn, but until this moment, he never knew what was missing in his life until he saw the doctor hold up their baby.

An hour after her birth, Dedrick had his little girl back in his arms and was headed down to the room where Jaclyn had been moved to after the delivery. Another nurse with a cradlette followed him, and once the door opened, Dedrick's private time with his little girl was over.

waiting for them, and with great reluctance, Dedrick went over to Jaclyn and handed her the baby. "Here you go, Mom."

Dedrick stood back and let the family get a peek at the newest member. Stefan put his arm around Dedrick's shoulder and smiled as the women made a fuss over the baby. Even the boys pushed their way in to get a better look.

"One of the greatest feelings in the world, isn't it?" Stefan asked with a grin.

"At one time, I never thought I would find my mate," Dedrick said. "Now I stand here with a little girl that I would give my life for in a heartbeat and a woman I love beyond words."

Dedrick smiled at Stefan and put his own arm around his shoulders. "Stefan, it doesn't get any better than this."

* * * *

Drake reached his hand out and touched his new cousin's head. Some strange thoughts came to his mind, but one thing screamed out. She didn't have a name yet. "What are you going to call her?"

"I don't know," Jaclyn answered. "I sort of expected a boy. What do you think I should name her?"

"Can I hold her?" Drake asked.

Jaclyn smiled. "Sure." Carefully she handed the tiny bundle to Drake who held her with such care.

"Look at her feet!" Brock snorted. "They're so tiny."

"You both used to have feet that small," Sidney told them, touching the baby's head.

"She's happy," Drake stated. He looked up at Stefan, who came up to the bed. "I can see inside her mind." He smiled and peeked back down at the baby, who now had her eyes open and a frown on her face. "Celine. You should call her Celine."

Dedrick came up to the bed and placed both hands on Drake's shoulders. "I think that is perfect, since she looked like her mother. Celine Elizabeth Draeger."

"Hello, CeeCee." Brock grinned. "Welcome to the family." Drake handed the baby to Brock and moved away from the bed.

While the family made a fuss over her, Drake went over to the window and stared out. He was changing inside. Could feel it. While he was thinking about what might be going on inside him, his eyes landed on a dark sedan parked away from the other cars in the parking lot. It wasn't a patient car, but his grandfather's car. He was watching them, waiting for another opening.

"Hey, buddy." Stefan knelt down next to him, his arm around his shoulders. "You okay?"

"I'm different," Drake told him. "Why am I different, Daddy?"

"You're not different, Drake. Why would you think that?" Stefan spoke quietly, like he always did when something was bothering Drake or Brock.

"Brock can't see in people's minds." Drake looked at his father with a frown. "Why can I?"

"I told you a long time ago that some shifter males can do that," Stefan answered. "And not all can. You can."

Drake turned back to the window and fixed his eyes on the dark car. He felt angry that they would be here, watching them. He was almost one when his grandfather took him, and he would never forget what they did to him. Drake could still feel it at night, the needle going into his back, and the rough hands holding him down. It was a nightmare that just wouldn't go away. Same as the headaches. Because of the shock treatments, he now suffered from migraines.

"They're coming again," Drake whispered. "And they want to do bad things."

"Drake?"

Drake turned and frowned at Stefan. "They're watching us again, and I'm afraid they're never going to stop."

Stefan looked out the window and stood up. Drake knew that he saw the dark car that was out of place in the parking lot. "Dedrick."

Drake looked again as Dedrick stood behind him. "It's not over," Drake whispered. "Not yet anyway." He turned to both Stefan and Dedrick. "But I'm going to get even. That's a promise."

www.jadensinclair.com
Interplanetary Passions
Outerplanetary Sensations
S.E.T.H.
S.H.I.L.O.
Lucifer's Lust, with Mae Powers
In the Shifter Series:
Book 1: Stefan's Mark
Book 2: Claiming Skyler
Book 3: Dedrick's Taming
Book 4: The Prowling
Book 5: Cole's Awakening
Book 6: The New Breed
Book 7: Seducing Sasha

The Prowling
By Jaden Sinclair

The Draeger brothers are a unique breed for one simple reason. They are identical twins. It is something that in the shifter world never happens. But where they might look alike in appearance their personalities differ.

Brock is funny, laid back and easy going were Drake is hard and dark. They balance each other out perfectly but the balance gets tipped when Drake gives into his vengeful side.

Together the brothers are a force to be reckoned with. They will do anything and everything to keep their family safe, but when they mate, a choice is laid before them. Give in to the hate, or give in to their hearts.

Lightning Source UK Ltd.
Milton Keynes UK
UKOW03f0402171216
290178UK00002B/445/P